Bait and Snitch

PONDEROSA PINES MYSTERIES
BOOK FOUR

REGINA WELLING

ERIN LYNN

Willow Hill BOOKS

Contents

Bait and Snitch

Prologue

This couldn't be happening. Alicia Kayden pushed back from her desk in a tiny cubicle at the very back of the first-floor offices of Levy & Wade, drummed her fingers on its polished surface, and frowned at her computer screen. A mistake. There was no other valid explanation. Some error in data entry, perhaps. Determined, she slid back even farther to snatch the hard copy from a table behind her desk.

No amount of leafing through the paperwork changed what she saw on the screen. Alicia's choice of an internal auditing concentration for her master's degree was certainly paying off, but no course had prepared her for the actuality of fraud. There was little doubt in her mind that a good chunk of this client's expenses were falsified, resulting in decreased tax liability; and there was zero doubt that a scheme of this magnitude could only have been perpetrated with inside help.

Hours later, eyes feeling like itchy marbles from time spent searching for something to prove what she'd seen was a mistake, Alicia admitted defeat. She hit print, gathered up the sheets as they appeared, and put them in the folder with the original data.

Dread dogged her movements. What she was about to show her boss would shake the firm's foundations and implicate a fellow accountant. Alicia had no idea how deep the deception went, and wasn't looking forward to finding out. The possibility that she could be treading into dangerous waters wasn't lost on her.

The sound of her heels tapping on the tile as her feet carried her into her boss's office was one she would never forget. It was the sound that marked the beginning of the end of Alicia Kayden.

Chapter 1

“ *Hey, Piniacs, are you ready to dish? Love is certainly in the air over Ponderosa Pines this Valentine's Day. Let's hope the Ericksons aren't too distracted with baby planning— all those happy couples out there are going require a truckload of chocolate covered strawberries. I'd bet Rhonda would appreciate a volunteer or two—and I'd also bet she'll be willing to throw in some glazed donuts as payment.*

Speaking of happy couples, I'm betting none of you are surprised that Inspector Hottie has been joined at the hip with his lifelong crush—we all saw it coming a mile away! Judging by the size of the rock she's carting around on her left hand, it won't be long before our 'Save the Date' cards arrive.

And ladies, if you're into law enforce-

ment officials, you might want to skip town to look for a Valentine: both our badges have been claimed. Deputy Dalton and Ms. Grapevine herself have finally given in; reports of their canoodling all over town are filling the tip line mailbox to overflowing. Enough already!

But that's not all—it seems a certain combat boot-sporting lady has won the heart of our favorite gardening guru. Tank's going to be strapped for time this month; juggling co-op classes, manning Winter Heating and Conservation tours, and keeping a new girl-friend happy besides. Good luck, buddy! Though I will say, she seems to be a good influence, judging by the rate Tank's losing his beer belly. Looking good!

Ah, yes, the WHaC is coming right up! Everyone get ready: the University is projecting its highest participation level of all time. Which, if you remember the horde of onlookers we entertained last year, means we'll have our hands full this time around. It seems we're looking at three daily tours of the Pines: three groups of strangers tramping down our streets; peeking into our backyards; and, best of all, spending money at our small businesses. Let's put our best face forward and show 'em what we've got!

As always, I expect the influx of fresh meat to put a spring in our favorite busty inn owner's step—will this be the year she finally meets her match? We'll all keep our eyes open for someone suitable, and send him your way, Ms. Calabrese.

In return, maybe Lottie will try to reign in her westerly neighbor—he's gone a bit overboard with the Posted signs. Nobody from the University is going to try to steal your lawn ornaments, Mr. Z.; relax and breathe. Let's try to come across as welcoming to our guests, and dial down the unnecessary crazy.

Finally, I'll be a busy little bee myself over the next few weeks, so keep those eyes open and the tips coming!

Chapter 2

"Psst, over here!" Chloe LaRue's hoarse whisper was barely audible over the din of clinking silverware and several other conversations going on inside the Mudbucket, but EV Torrence spotted her friend the instant she passed through the door. Considering Chloe was the only one in the room wearing a head scarf and dark-rimmed sunglasses, she was hard to miss.

"Why, hello, Miss Monroe, fancy meeting you here." EV teased as she settled into a brightly painted chair across from Chloe. The eye roll behind Chloe's sunglasses was nearly audible to EV—and she had expected no less. Chloe tossed her shoulder-length blond hair and scrunched her slightly upturned button nose in EV's direction.

"You keep it up and your face will get stuck like that. You'll have to spend the rest of your life looking at the insides of your eyelids."

"Ha ha. You're hilarious." Chloe slid the glasses up on her head, thought better of a second eye roll, and trained her wide chocolate-colored eyes on EV's face with effort. Sable hair hung in layers around EV's high, flushed cheekbones, and framed bright, sparkling green eyes. It was easy to see why people never believed EV was in her '50's; she exemplified how clean eating and regular exercise could slow the ravages of age.

EV grinned. "It's all right, I felt like I had to sneak around to get here, too. I took a seriously roundabout route through the woods and the east field. The fairy garden is not a peaceful place when you're snow-shoeing through it. Killed two birds with one stone, though, and got in my workout for the day!"

Now that Nate Harper was shacking up at Chloe's house, and EV had claimed half of Dalton Burnsoll's dresser drawers, the two best friends' nightly wanderings through the backyard path between their houses had decreased to infrequent at best. Both men would have understood the need for them to make time for each other, but it was much more fun to meet up like this—away from prying eyes and ears.

Sure, the clandestine nature of their time together may have been noticed by other residents of

Ponderosa Pines, but it wasn't something Chloe would be commenting on in her column, 'Babble & Spin'. Nobody in town—save for EV and, of course, Nate—knew the identity of the mystery author, and this was one of those times Chloe would stoop to use the anonymity to her advantage. Reporting on her own relationships always made Chloe uncomfortable, but sometimes there was no way around it; no mention of herself or her close friends would arouse suspicion in the long run.

A town like Ponderosa Pines—boasting just over 500 residents, many of whom were descendants of the original 60's commune from which the hamlet had risen—thrived on gossip of any kind. EV's unofficial position as matriarch allowed her access to a bevy of information, and caused a contingent of townspeople to wonder whether she was responsible for the installment of snark printed in *The Pine Cone* each week. Not that she didn't contribute; but passing tidbits to Chloe for follow-up was as big a part as she wanted to play.

"So how is Nate adjusting to life in your itty bitty house?" EV asked with interest. Before Chloe could answer, an ever-expanding Rhonda Erickson waddled over to their table and barked, uncharacter-istically, "What'll it be?" at the back of EV's head.

Spinning around in her chair, EV surveyed the pregnant woman and immediately rose to offer her aching feet a break. "Sit, now." She commanded before marching around the curved counter to make her own mocha cappuccino.

"I'm sorry, EV. Didn't mean to bite your head off. This baby is going to be fifteen pounds if he keeps growing like this. David's out picking up some supplies to finish the nursery, and the last hour has felt like five, at least." She rolled her neck back and forth, pinching the bridge of her nose as if to stave off an oncoming headache.

"No problem, I still remember how to steam milk. Did I ever tell you I helped Dalton out a few times when he owned the place? Marlene felt about like you do right before she had Carrie, so I pulled a few shifts while they looked for someone to replace her."

"Well, thanks for giving me a minute to catch my breath. That mocha is on me; Chloe's too. I'm sure I'll see you ladies in here tomorrow for another private chat." A quick wink let EV know that Rhonda had noticed their seemingly-innocent increase in caffeine cravings, but wouldn't share their secret with anyone else.

"You call me when you have that baby; I'm volunteering to lend a hand. All it will cost you is a few baby cuddles." With no children of her own, EV's only chance at sniffing baby heads came vicariously. With Chloe and Nate all snugged up, she was hoping for a pink or blue bundle to come along soon. Auntie EV had a nice ring to it, and was the only tolerable option. Calling EV by her given name of Emmalina was a big no-no, and being referred to as Auntie Em was simply out of the question.

Rhonda smiled ruefully and patted her stomach. "If he ever decides to come out, I'll let you know."

"Do you have any family coming in for the happy event?" Rhonda wasn't one to talk about her family, which sparked Chloe's innate curiosity. "Both Inns are probably booked up by now, but I bet EV would be happy to bunk with Dalton and give up her place if a bed is needed." Chloe raised her voice so EV, who bustled around clearing tables and serving coffee, could hear her.

"Happy to." EV assured.

"Our folks all live up in the county—four, maybe five-hour drive depending on road conditions. Doc

Talbot says first babies always take a while, so we figured they'd all have time to get here once things start to roll. Mom says she's been going to bed fully dressed in case the call comes in the middle of the night." Rhonda grinned at the mental picture. "They'd have all been here and underfoot for the past week if I'd given the word. I'm already hormonal, I don't need a house full of well-meaning parents at the moment. But I think I'll take you up on that offer when the time comes if you're serious, EV."

"Just say the word." EV settled back in her seat. "So, Mata Hari, where's that seed catalog you promised to bring? Nothing like picking out flowers when it's threatening to snow."

Chloe plopped said catalog onto the table, fully a quarter of the page corners were turned down indicating they held items she was interested in planting. Alongside the catalog, she unfolded a sheet of graph paper with detailed outlines of what she planned for the year. By the time all her final choices had been penciled in, the threat of snow had become a reality.

. . .

"A chocolate chip cookie? A chicken head? A needle threader?" EV shouted excitedly, a loud beeping noise cutting off the last guess.

"It was the Millennium Falcon!" Dalton cried over the sound of exuberant laughter filling Chloe's tiny living room. Curly dark hair with only a touch of gray at the temples framed eyes that grew laugh lines every time Dalton flashed the smile that took him from cute to handsome. Tall and rangy with not even an ounce of pretension, he was EV's perfect match even if it had taken her half a lifetime to realize it.

As Chloe picked up a scrap of paper containing the next clue, she surveyed the room full of loved ones and felt her heart swell with happiness. Game night was becoming a Friday evening tradition, with all of her favorite people gathered in one place. Tonight's edition they dubbed the 'Almost Blizzard Bowl' since the predicted heavy snowfall had not yet materialized. What was coming down now might have been considered excessive in other parts of the country, but here it was just par for the course.

Veronica, whose voluptuous figure barely evidenced the five children she had birthed, leaned against her husband, Franklin, her face radiating contentment as she absently stroked his arm. Cornflower blue eyes looked up through thick, lowered lashes as her ruby lips stretched into a beguiling smile. Veronica's wild days were behind her —and she had been adventurous to the extreme— and now it was rare to catch her without at least a couple of children clamoring for her attention, or without Mindy, the fourth woman of the group.

Mindy's petite, sylphlike frame belied the yoga and kickboxing-gleaned strength that lay underneath, as did the mischievous smile that she nearly always wore. Mindy, a typical redhead, could go from zero to sixty in about 2.2 seconds. She cast occasional glances at her longtime boyfriend, Jace, who was deep in conversation with Nate across the room.

"V, you're up after me." Chloe tossed the comment over her shoulder and proceeded to draw a bird-like shape and what appeared to be a pile of spaghetti, and watched recognition pass over Nate's face before he correctly guessed 'One Flew Over the Cuckoo's Nest' to her delight. None of the dozens of jobs Chloe had held throughout her thirty-three years had, thankfully, required any level of measurable artistic talent beyond an eye for shape and color.

EV and Dalton, with twenty more years of experience than the rest of the group, were the clear front-runners for the win. It didn't hurt that, save for knitting, EV excelled at just about everything, or that Franklin's tendency toward making questionable guesses thwarted Veronica's superior artistic skills. When, with an economy of line, she rendered a spot-on image of George Washington, Franklin swore it was Indiana Jones.

"And this is for the win," EV took a look at the yellow block on her card and her face flushed a dull red. With swift strokes, she sketched out a series of stacked shapes.

"Blocks? A pyramid?" Dalton called out. EV shook her head. On the top, she roughed out a very hastily drawn stick couple. "Wedding cake?" She added a dress and veil then an arrow pointing toward the male half. "Groom? Husband?" Dalton nailed it half a second before time ran out. He accepted EV's elated high five, then quietly tore the sheet of paper from the oversize tablet, folded it into a bulky square, and stashed it in his pocket.

. . .

"I think they think they're getting away with something, sneaking out to the shed for cigars and man time." Mindy commented with a smirk once the men had vacated and the women were ensconced in the kitchen, sipping wine and laughing like teenagers.

"Let them keep thinking so." EV replied. "Never underestimate the value of the upper hand. Though, to be fair, I'm probably not the authority on how to treat husbands or *boyfriends*, seeing as I haven't been in a long-term relationship for quite some time. By the way, what is a woman in her fifties supposed to call a man anyway? Boyfriend sounds so juvenile..."

"Stud Muffin?" Chloe piped up from her cross-legged position on the kitchen island. When the laughter died down, she continued, "Don't ask me; one of the first thoughts I had after Nate proposed was *thank goodness, I can call him my fiancé now*. Min, what about you—what do you call Jace?"

"I hate to say it, but boyfriend is the best option. You use 'partner', and you have people wondering if you're talking about business, or assuming you're in a same sex relationship. Personally, I don't care what people think, but what I can't stand is the eyebrows that remain raised—either literally or implied—until you clarify with a gender-specific pronoun."

"Companion conjures images of old British ladies for some ungodly reason." Veronica mused. "Beau would be better, but it's so uncommon in the north—and in this decade, for that matter."

"Just don't call him your boo." Chloe teased lightly, trying to imagine the word 'boo' passing EV's lips. "Or your bae. Which, according to social media, is short for 'baby' because apparently that last syllable is too much." She rolled her eyes. "Pretty soon we'll all be speaking in shorthand."

Distaste shot EV's eyebrows up at the word bae. Never. Not ever would that word pass her lips.

Veronica threw an arm around EV's neck and leaned in conspiratorially. "Pretty soon you won't have this problem anyway. Anyone can see where this is headed. According to *Babble & Spin*, you and Dalton ought to be making an announcement anytime now."

Chloe's eyes widened imperceptibly at the reference to her column; she wished she could share her identity with Veronica and Mindy. Chloe firmly believed that secrecy in any form was detrimental to otherwise meaningful relationships, and feared this particular withholding placed a metaphorical wedge in her friendship with the women.

"Believing everything you read in *Babble & Spin* is about the same as basing political opinions on Facebook memes." A small snort escaped Chloe's lips, which EV studiously ignored.

Over the previous twenty-four hours, meteorologists had christened the blizzard crawling up the east coast with a name. Winter Storm Tilly was now swirling her snowy skirts through the mighty Atlantic, picking up even more ammunition for when she would finally unleash her fury on the state of Maine. Due the day before, Tilly had decided on a fashionably late entrance, in typical feminine fashion.

Attorney Stacey Hawthorne heard the reports, and knew darned well this was absolutely the wrong time to travel. Even the few miles between her office on the farthest edge of the Gilmore town limits and the sleepy village of Ponderosa Pines. But this couldn't wait; her best guess was that this recent turn of events could be matter of life and death.

It had all started when she received a call from a former colleague to tell her about Ronald Trafton's untimely death, and then had come Alicia's shocked assertion that being deathly afraid of heights, Ronald would never have gone up on that roof of his own accord. Putting those two pieces of information together pulled Stacey's mind down a path that led to her driving through the treacherous darkness of a snow-covered road when she should have been curled up on the sofa next to her cat.

"Remain on the current road in 2 miles."

"Why? Why would you say that, GPS wench?" She said out loud, though she was alone in the car. "Telling me when NOT to turn isn't helpful." Stacey's nerves were stretched to breaking, having spent most of an hour hunched over the steering wheel, attempting to see past the stubby end of the hood. She'd flicked on the GPS, though she knew the route well, in hopes of utilizing the map feature to prepare for upcoming bends in a road she could barely see. Even with all-wheel drive, the trip was quickly heading into what-was-I-thinking territory. Stacey glanced over at the sheaf of papers on the passenger's seat and sighed.

With several ongoing cases involving people from Ponderosa Pines, driving over ahead of the storm had made sense. It was the time spent getting everything in order that was now coming back to bite her in the butt. She probably should have listened to the guy at the gas station when he told her to turn back. Oh well, too late now. And, with any luck, the storm would slow down the trouble following behind her.

"Remain on the current road in 1.5 miles."

The GPS voice was meant to be soothing and instructive, but instead it just flat got on Stacey's nerves. The ding ding sound to signal a turn, in her opinion, should be reserved only for those times when a turn was necessary. Less confusion all around, and fewer instances where a lack of meticulous attention might lead to a wrong turn. She, of course, would never be guilty of doing such a thing. Sure.

Ding Ding.

Stacey remained, as instructed, on the current road. Not that there had actually been a turn anyway. She was pretty sure the gadget had come equipped with the you-can't-get-there-from-here option, since it constantly advised her to take turns down dirt tracks that even the longest stretch of the imagination couldn't call actual roads.

She imagined how satisfying it would be to rip the annoying piece of electronic garbage from her dash and toss it out the window, wires trailing behind like severed limbs, but settled for the precarious act of taking one hand off the wheel to punch the mute button. It proved to be a huge mistake as the car crested a hill. For a split second, the wind died down enough to let her see the slope ahead. It was steeper than expected and, within seconds, downward momentum pulled the car into a slide. Berating herself for being distracted over such a trivial matter, Stacey whipped the wheel and promptly overcompensated. In a panic, she spiked the brakes instead of pulsing them, and the slide devolved into a spin. Before she had time to think straight, the car started to careen down the hill like a pinball bouncing off a set of rubber bumpers.

Under her feet, the floor vibrated with the sound of snow whooshing past. Two hard bumps pushed her painfully against the seat belt and then against the door before the car jolted to a stop on the other side of a two-foot snowbank. Great. Here she was, less than half a mile from town. So close, but without a tow truck, there was no way her car would be taking her on that journey.

Reaching for her purse, Stacey found it had flown off the seat during the debacle. its contents littered the floor: pens, a lipstick, nail clippers, coins, her wallet, half a dozen business cards, and a small notepad. Unbuckling the seat belt, she flipped on the dome light in the still idling car, leaned over to retrieve her files and her cell phone from where they had wedged between the passenger's seat and the door.

Hoping against hope that she would have enough bars to make a call—something that was never a given in the more rural areas of the state—Stacey called her insurance company to arrange a tow. The sympathetic, but less than helpful voice on the other end informed her it would be at least a day, maybe two given the storm, before anyone would come for her car. Stacey contemplated dialing 9-1-1 and, instead, searched her phone for Alicia's number. After seven rings, she hung up. There was one other number to try, then she would just have to give in and make the trek into town. No answer. Where was everyone? Shouldn't they be at home by now, huddled up with a loaf of bread and a gallon of milk? Stacey had never understood the mentality of stocking up on those particular items before a storm, but now envied those who were now warm, dry, and prepared.

Given the horror stories of people dying in their cars while snow covered the exhaust to direct carbon monoxide back into the vehicle, staying here in the warmth generated by her heater was not an option. Good thing she had at least worn warm clothing. Judging everything else would be safe for a day or two, she pocketed her cell phone and wallet, and was reaching forward to switch off the ignition when she heard a knock right next to her head. Stacey breathed a sigh of relief at the unexpected rescue.

Condensation coated the inside of the window, making it difficult to see the face looking in at her. The relief from seconds before disappeared as a rush of foreboding whispered over Stacey, making her shiver. A dark country road might not be the best place for meeting new people. She left the car running and keyed the window down.

"Are you hurt?" The man's face was half covered by a hat pulled down low over his eyes and a collar he'd turned up against the wind.

"I'm fine. I've already called for a tow truck." It wasn't a lie, even if one would not be coming anytime soon.

"You'll have a long wait." His voice sounded familiar to her even though she couldn't see enough of his face to put a name to it. "I'm surprised you had cell service out here. Why don't you let me give you a ride, Ms. Hawthorne?"

Her name falling from his lips sent an instant chill through Stacey. Trained to observe and remember details in even the most trying circumstances, she knew for a fact that she had not mentioned her name.

"Who are you? I never told you my name."

He leaned in closer and Stacey gasped as her dome light illuminated his face. "You. How did you find me?"

"People who really want to hide don't just move back home. Where's Alicia? Or whatever she's calling herself these days."

"How did you find out about her?"

"You'd be surprised how much information you can get out of a cop on the take. Tell me where she is."

"I can't do that." Fear turned Stacey's bones to liquid ice.

"Oh, but you will. Now get out of the car." He pulled the door open and when she didn't immediately exit, yanked her out into the snow, hands pulling cruelly at her hair. "Don't fight me on this." His order had the opposite effect. Stacey went into wildcat mode, kicking and clawing at him. She landed a solid elbow to his face. Blood welled out of his nose to drip onto the pristine white snow. Shock slackened his hold on her long enough to give her a clear shot at kicking him in the misters. At the last minute he swiveled, and the kick went wide.

When he pulled the gun out of his pocket, Stacey went instantly still, a new level of fear calling a surge of adrenaline into her veins.

"I don't want to have to shoot you, Ms. Hawthorne. That would be messy. Do yourself a favor and tell me where to find Alicia."

The temptation to do just that rose to pull at her, while her desire to protect Alicia did the same. He took a step forward and she felt the cold, hard steel slide through her hair, nudge hard against her temple.

"Tell me where she is."

Living alone in the city and working for the DA were both good reasons to take a few self-defense classes. Remembering her training, Stacey ignored the sound of her heart hammering in her ears and, moving as quickly as she could, raised her hand to push the gun back toward him. The element of surprise Raoul preached at every class ticked through her brain: never pull a gun toward you, because the reflex on the trigger could make it go off; pushing it straight back gave the best chance for disarming an attacker, or buying some time, anyway.

It worked, too. Grunting in surprise, he dropped the gun. Stacey went limp and fell to the ground. She fumbled for the weapon, but instead of turning it on him—the odds against him retaking control were too high—she whipped it as far as she could into the darkness and falling snow.

The cloud of white flakes muffled his angry growl.

They grappled furiously until his hands settled on her throat.

"Where is she?"

Eyes wide, Stacey shook her head. There was just enough light coming from the car to let her see the set lines on his face through the shifting curtain of swirling snow. If she gave him what he wanted, Alicia was dead. Worse, the look in his eye said Alicia wouldn't be the only one. She clamped her lips closed and shook her head; he responded with a frustrated shake, and she could feel something hard—probably a rock—tap against the back of her head.

"Tell me." He went from cold calculation to hot

fury in the blink of an eye. His hands tightened on her throat, his body pressed her further into whatever lay beneath the snow.

It was too late for her now and she knew it. The world grayed around the edges and then went black.

Chapter 4

Christian West's ears perked when he heard a series of shushing noises followed by a thump that was louder than any sound snow might make falling from a tree branch. Off to his right and thirty feet down a steep embankment, route 15 took a nasty turn at the bottom of Elbow Hill. Orienting his attention toward the sound, Christian began the task of picking his way safely down toward the road. If not for the whirling snow, he would have had a birds-eye view of the accident. Instead, he could only rely on his ears to tell the story. The trail he was on ran along Huff Ridge, and the way down would take him through some rough terrain, but Christian would not be deterred if he thought someone might need help.

His evening trek through the snowy woods around the northern edge of Ponderosa Pines had become a ritual of sorts—even in stormy weather.

Sure, the entire town was fairly remote, and boasted a number of trails and secluded locations, but this particular end remained close to his heart. Several months earlier, after suffering a head injury, Christian had secretly lived in an abandoned camp site close by. His overgrown appearance and night-time wanderings had the Pines believing a Sasquatch had taken up residence in their beloved woods.

Upon discovery that he was, indeed, just a man—and a gentle-souled one at that—the town as a whole had embraced his presence and offered him a small cabin and a chance to become part of the community. The invitation had touched Christian's heart, and he couldn't help wanting to learn more about the loving, if somewhat odd, group of people who made up Ponderosa Pines. As such, he felt a certain amount of civic duty, which compelled him to regularly monitor the acres of forest surrounding his home.

In his present state, he resembled a Yeti more than a Sasquatch. Snow clung to the fibers of his shaggy wool coat and hat. Something about the wild nature of the wind had called to him—or maybe it was just a sixth sense that brought him out into the howling white darkness on this night. Unlike Stacey, he appreciated his GPS—probably because it never talked back to him—a handheld model with a backlit display that would guide him home in the worst a storm could offer. Right now, he checked his position, then tucked it back into his jacket pocket where it rested alongside his cell phone, and pulled out the pair of night vision goggles that had been a gift from a new friend. With the idea of becoming either a game warden or wilderness guide—whichever one gave him the best chance of being included in search and rescue missions—he'd been training himself to move through the night woods without their aid by sharpening his senses of hearing and smell.

There were only three places where the lay of the land would allow him to make his way down from the hill. One was half a mile behind him, and more difficult than the other two. The second of the three, marked by a splash of red paint on the bark of a silver birch tree, was coming up around the next bend. Moving into the loping sort of jog that was the fastest he could move in snowshoes, Christian's eyes scanned for the mark that would only show as a minor change in color under the green vision he saw through the glasses. He almost missed it despite his vigilance. The snowshoes were almost more hindrance than help on the downward slope, but he managed anyway.

Closer now, he heard a second vehicle, the slamming of a car door, muffled voices, and shortly thereafter, tires spinning for purchase in the snow-covered road. It sounded like the drama was over, but it wasn't in his nature to turn back without at least making sure.

What he couldn't understand was what anyone would be doing out on the road on a night like this. While a snowstorm—even one as bad as this—wasn't enough to force everyone inside, this road, a secondary one leading to Gilmore, was the last place Christian expected to see any traffic tonight. With each passing second the sense of urgency strengthened. Someone might have taken an unfortunate turn on the road ahead. February was the coldest month of the year, and winter weather warnings and advisories had been in effect for the better part of the week.

Now, with Tilly drifting her slow way northwest, nearly a foot of snow had accumulated in a matter of hours, and the deluge showed no sign of lessening anytime soon. Anyone passing through must either be from out of town, or have a legitimate reason to brave the treacherous roads. Maybe Rhonda Erickson had gone into labor and David was trying to get her to the hospital. His step quickened as the familiar feeling that someone was in trouble pressed in on him harder, and he knew he was the only one who might be able to help. He wouldn't allow for anything less—not this time.

The muffled rumble of an idling car cut through the noise of wind and the shush of falling snow.

Christian cut through a break in the trees, deep drifts of snow slowing his progress. He knew the road curved at a sharp angle and on a downward trajectory where it snaked through the forest up ahead. That was the most likely spot for an accident, and from where he was sure the noise had originated. He picked up the pace, by now thankful he had strapped on the crude pair of snowshoes that made navigating the section of tightly packed snowfall much less difficult.

Finally, he reached the embankment marking the edge of the road; this area wouldn't see a plow until tomorrow given the weather conditions. It was already a seldom-traveled stretch of dirt road, and one of the last plowed during heavy storms. A single sliver of headlight, muted by the shifting curtain of snow, beamed from the ditch on the opposite side of the road. Christian's daily jogs along winding country paths had increased his endurance, and he barely struggled for breath when he ripped off the snowshoes and broke into a full run toward the wreck.

As he approached the vehicle, it became clear that the driver had lost control, gone into a spin, and wound up in the ditch, but at a speed slow enough that loss of life seemed an unlikely possibility. Relief flooded his senses until he rounded the driver's side of the still running car and, in the meager light that spilled from the open door, noticed a patch of blood spattered across the white expanse of snow. Trepidation filled him when he saw a woman sprawled lifelessly across the center console.

Christian briefly wondered how blood could have ended up outside the car if her injuries had been sustained during the crash. The logical part of his brain noted a set of footprints leading in the other direction from the ones he had created on his approach. Straining his neck to see over the bank, he saw a set of deeply etched marks left by spinning tires and the deep grooves continuing on toward Ponderosa Pines. Every minute detail etched itself into his memory as he gently turned toward what he hoped was not a dead body inside the car. Shaking fingers tested for the delicate flutter at the base of her throat. Unconscious, but still breathing, her pulse was strong. Christian felt a profound sense of relief.

"My name is Christian, and I'm here to help you."

Moving carefully, he hit the lever to tilt the seat back all the way back, and keeping her neck and head supported, cradled the woman's body to roll her off the console and into a more comfortable position on the seat. Christian shed his coat, shook off the layer of snow, and laid it over her for the extra warmth. Angry red shading to purple marred the otherwise smooth column of her throat, and a trickle of blood stained her temple where a large knot stood out in stark relief against her auburn hair.

When he stepped back, he felt something under his foot. Reaching down, he fished a red leather wallet out of the snow where his boot had pressed it down.

"Ma'am, I found your wallet, I'm going to open it so I can look at your identification." There was no response, but the sound of his own voice soothed Christian's pounding heart, so he kept up a steady stream of words meant to convince her he was there to help. Fingers beginning to tremble from the rush of adrenaline, he pulled the license from her wallet.

As Christian looked down into Stacey Hawthorne's face his world tilted; spun into peaceful darkness for a split second before returning to normal. Only now, everything was in high-definition; something had clicked into place, something he hadn't been able to get a handle on before. He didn't know why or how, but he felt connected to this woman; as if she were a close friend instead of a complete stranger, and knew that he desperately wanted her to open her eyes and survive. Christian held Stacey's hand while he dialed for help, and prayed.

"If it keeps up like this, the doomsayers might be right about this being one of the worst storms of the decade, and that's saying a lot." EV murmured, peering through the curtains at the swirling flakes outside. "I can't even see Bert and Celia's porch light, and they leave it on 24/7."

Most of the houses in Ponderosa Pines were set apart from their neighbors, but this section of town was the first to have been established. In its conception as a commune, close proximity made sense, and fostered the spirit of cooperative habitation. Decades later, the landscape now featured several culs-de-sac branching off Main Street where it came to a dead end at the edge of the forest. Here, where EV and Chloe's homes sat, trails wound through each yard and into the acres of surrounding woods, providing foot access to almost every part of town.

"I know!" Chloe bounded over and pressed her own nose to the glass. "It's wild! I remember Mom telling me about some pretty crazy nor'easters, but I always thought she was being a little dramatic." I haven't seen anything like this since I've been back. It's kind of awesome, actually. Good thing we don't need to go out for anything!"

"Remember this the next time you're making fun of my stockpiling habits. It's not just preparation for the zombie apocalypse—anything could happen, and now you know how nice it feels to be prepared." EV elbowed Chloe in the ribs, satisfaction coaxing a wide grin to her face. Chloe would have no choice but to couch this particular diatribe; in fact, EV would be willing to bet her friend was making a mental list of survival supplies for her next trip to Costco.

"Did someone say zombie apocalypse?" Dalton

called from EV's living room where he and Nate were enjoying an old basketball game on ESPN Classic.

"Yes, but don't worry; we're safe for now." EV chuckled, motioning for Chloe to follow her out of the kitchen.

"Nice shorts." Chloe snorted, casting a glance at the television as she settled into an oversize Suzani armchair next to Nate. "I'm glad that '80's trend has yet to return."

Dalton's cheeks reddened; he knew there was a nearly identical pair of short shorts in his bottom dresser drawer, leftover from the offending decade. He'd keep that bit of information to himself, thank-you-very-much.

EV set a plate of fresh-baked brownies on the coffee table and everyone dug in. "Can't even tell I replaced the oil with a mashed banana, can you?" she asked, already knowing the answer.

"Does that make them count as fruit? Chocolate has antioxidants, so that sounds like health food to me!" Nate chimed.

"Sounds logical, let's go with that." Dalton mumbled through a full mouth. EV bent over to give him a crumb-covered kiss.

Nate had just slugged back half a glass of milk

when his cell phone sounded, interrupting the feeling of contentment in which all four of them had enjoyed basking. "This is Nate." His brow furrowed as he listened intently, and he shot Dalton an urgent look.

"We'll be right there." He barked, then hung up the phone. "Christian West. There's been an accident out on route 15. A woman named Stacey Hawthorne went off the road at the bottom of Elbow Hill. Ambulance is en route with a snow plow assist from the Gilmore end. Let's see what we can do to make things easier on our end."

Dalton was already shrugging into his jacket while EV picked up the phone to make a call. In under a minute, she had lined up three locals with plow trucks. Tank Daniels would pick up Doc Talbot on the way. "Is there anything else you can tell us?"

"Christian found her almost immediately, but he said there's more to it. Looks like she's been assaulted. We've got to get out there and check out the scene before it's covered in snow."

"I'll drive." Dalton said, his face grave. Stacey had been the one to handle Marlene's side of the divorce. She'd been sympathetic but fair, and he respected her for that.

The two quickly donned hats, gloves, and boots, kissed Chloe and EV and headed out into the billowing storm.

"I hope she's all right; Stacey is a lovely woman. I can't imagine why she'd be out driving in this weather though." Unsettled, EV paced over to the window again to stare out into the darkness, worry etched in the frown lines between her eyes.

"I'm not sure I know who she is."

"She's a lawyer with Steinke, Burns, and Pruitt over in Gilmore—general practice. She helped me set up the grant for the Ericksons. Since then, I've seen her in town a couple of times. About your age, very pretty, always pleasant. I can't imagine why anyone would want to hurt her."

Chloe's eyes narrowed. "Maybe it was random. Though, that's possibly more concerning. Either way, there's someone running around here who doesn't balk at beating on women. Are you getting that tingly feeling?"

"You mean like there might be another mystery for us to solve?"

"Exactly. You still running chains on Christine's tires?" Chloe asked, referring to EV's old, beat-up Chevy truck—a rusty relic with a heart of purest steel, Christine could bull her way through just about anything.

"Of course, get your coat."

"You know we're going to receive death glares from the guys for this, right?" Chloe asked, grinning from ear to ear. She didn't have enough fingers and toes to count the number of times Nate and Dalton had told them to stay out of official police business, so why start listening now?

EV put the truck in gear and gunned the engine, earning a glare of her own from Chloe, who did not appreciate EV's driving style, even though her own Mini Cooper was covered in dings and dents from various objects Chloe claimed had 'come out of nowhere'.

"Don't be such a wimp. I know every pothole in town. And I'm positive they all know *you*." Such was the nature of their relationship. EV and Chloe's mother, Lila, had grown up together, and when Chloe moved back to Ponderosa Pines over three years ago, EV figured she'd take on a motherly role in Chloe's life. Instead, EV's youthfulness and Chloe's maturity had them both parked squarely in the middle of the twenty-year age gap, resulting in a deep, rock-steady friendship.

Christine's wipers whipped back and forth across the windshield, powdery flakes piling up again and clouding the view before they had even made a full pass. EV quickly but carefully maneuvered the ancient pickup through town, past the now-silent main block of quaint shops, and took a sharp right onto the road leading north out of Ponderosa Pines. Going on seven-thirty in the evening, the sun had set a good two and a half hours ago, and EV couldn't help but wonder why Stacey had been out in such low visibility.

Both women were silent as they approached the scene. Nate and Dalton looked up, their faces a mirror of each other as recognition turned to irritation.

"Aaaaand, there it is."

"Oh well, too late now. Here they come."

Nate flung open the passenger side door. "What are you two doing here?"

"Well, you didn't specifically tell us we couldn't come. We wanted to make sure Stacey was okay, and to check on Christian." Chloe shot back, her gaze not quite meeting Nate's eyes.

"Right, because you're such altruists. Nothing whatsoever to do with the fact that you're two of the nosiest people on the face of the planet." He spat back.

"And that you love the undying adoration you receive from the entire town because of it. Everyone at The Mudbucket will be clamoring for your attention tomorrow when they find out you were here." Dalton contributed, casting an annoyed glance at EV.

EV waved the accusation away impatiently. "Are you going to keep yelling at us, or tell us what's going on? You wouldn't have wanted us to risk our lives for nothing, now, would you? And we do want to check on poor Christian. Is Stacey going to be all right?"

Dalton sighed and exchanged another glance with Nate before launching into the details. "It's all going to come out anyway. She lost control on the hill and skidded over the bank. From what we can tell, she took no damage during the crash. Christian got to her about fifteen minutes after that. Sometime in between, she left the car and was assaulted. The strange part is, whoever hurt her tossed her back into the car and kept going toward town. It looks like he left her for dead."

Any tire mark evidence had been obliterated by snowplows and more falling snow.

"We can't get a definitive tread mark, so we have no idea what kind of vehicle it was. Christian said there was some blood in the snow, so we're going to see if we can recover any DNA and hope some of it's his."

"But what about Stacey?" Something told Chloe it wasn't looking good, otherwise that would have been the first thing out of Dalton's mouth.

Nate shook his head sadly. "She took a pretty bad blow to the head, and there are bruises and abrasions around her neck. Whoever did this choked her and banged her head on something. Maybe a hard piece of ice or a rock buried in the snow. She was unconscious when the ambulance took her. We're not sure whether she's going to make it or not."

"And where's Christian?" EV demanded.

"He went with her in the ambulance. The poor man looked like he'd seen a ghost, and he wouldn't let go of her hand the whole time. See, there was no need for you to come out here. We would have filled you in when we got back. Now go back home and let us finish up here."

Chloe, thinking on her feet, responded quickly. "If

you really want us out of the way that badly, we'll make the drive back to town. The two of us. Alone. In an old, rickety truck. Alone." She looked pointedly at Nate, whose deep blue eyes bugged momentarily as he realized the lengths she would go to in order to get her way. Chloe couldn't help thinking, even at a moment like this, how adorable her fiancée was—dark, slightly curly hair curled around his ears, drawing her eye toward his strong, sexy jawline and full, soft lips.

"Fine. Wait for us, and we'll all go together. But you stay on this side of the line. We can't have you contaminating anything." He turned on his heel and steered Dalton back through the mounting snow toward the immobile vehicle. When his back was turned, EV shot Chloe a thumbs up and proceeded to follow as far as they were allowed.

As the Crime Scene Unit arrived and processed the scene, Chloe and EV maneuvered around to the side of Stacey's car, careful to remain on the other side of the boundary marked with bright yellow tape, and found a vantage point facing directly into the passenger-side door.

EV squinted into the dark. "It's too far; I can't see anything clearly." She turned on her heel and marched back to the truck, throwing a quick "hold on" over her shoulder to Chloe, who watched as EV reached into the extended cab of the truck.

"Here," she said, handing Chloe a pair of night vision binoculars.

Chloe grinned. "And we thought we'd only use these to chase off the Sasq-Watchers!" She exclaimed, referring to the group of Sasquatch enthusiasts who invaded town after too many sightings of Christian in his unkempt state had leaked onto the Internet. EV and Chloe were forced to scare them out of town with a whack-a-doodle plan that included half the town.

"I see something that looks like a piece of paper. Just there by the door; must have fallen off the seat. Maybe she was on the clock." Chloe whispered.

"Maybe, but that looks an awful lot like an overnight bag in her back seat. I wonder where she was headed. Too bad we can't get a look at what's on that sheet of paper."

"I've got an idea. Hang on." Chloe pulled out her cell phone and tapped a quick text to both Lottie Calabrese and Sabra Pruitt—proprietors of the two inns located in Ponderosa Pines. "If she was planning to stay at either Open House or the Come On Inn, they'd know it." Seconds later, both women had replied in the negative, and with pleas for more information.

"Well, she didn't have reservations at either place. That could mean she was planning on staying with a friend."

"Or that she knew neither of those places is ever booked solid and didn't call ahead."

Chloe rolled her eyes. "Or that. But at least it's a place to start."

Chapter 5

For lack of any other reason than she wanted the exercise, EV strapped on snowshoes for her trip to knitting group. The hunk of ugly in her knitting bag was going to turn Priscilla's face a lovely shade of purple. What wanted to become a pair of boot toppers for Chloe looked more like pink Muppet roadkill.

Even worse, the group planned to choose a name for themselves today. EV, being the lone member against the idea, was not only voted down, but now forced to choose between several options—each one worse than the last. Ponderosa Pines Knitters was a mouthful. Stitch In Time didn't do anything for her either—that one had been done to death, really. The Needlers seemed slightly mean. The only option EV felt remotely acceptable was Knit Wits, but if she wasn't there to vote, she knew Lottie Calabrese would push for Knitpickers which was EV's least favorite choice. Not that it didn't fit Lottie to a T.

Soothed by the snowshoe's shushing noises and energized by the exercise, EV felt like the forest held its breath just for her. Every shade of blue painted the crystal sky and snow-laden shadows. Trees laboring under deceptively heavy clouds of white bent down to the ground as though they knelt in prayer. She found it hard not to believe in some form of divine providence with this kind of beauty in the world. As though in answer to that thought, a spear of sunlight slanted between two of the tallest sentinels to turn the world into a glittering wonder.

Breath pluming ahead of her, EV hated to leave nature's cathedral for the mundane world.

Of course, pulling off the foot gear made her late, though, given her history, EV congratulated herself for arriving slightly earlier than normal. Late or early, there was already a lively discussion going on behind the door leading to the back room of Thread.

"You can't name us Knitpickers. It makes us sound like a bunch of harpies. At least go with something a little more flattering," Chloe's voice rang out. Since she'd decided to come out of her shell and make herself heard, she'd been doing a bang-up job of it all over town.

"This was my idea; I should get to choose the name," Lottie's sharp tone grated on EV's nerves even from a distance. The woman had her moments, and then there were times like these when she used her voice as a weapon. EV was tempted to stand back and let Chloe take Lottie on single-handedly. That wouldn't be at all cowardly, even if Chloe could handle it.

She had just about decided to sneak back out and nip into The Mudbucket for a coffee when, for the first time ever, she heard Talia Plunkett agree with her sister. "I like Knitpickers. I mean, we knit and we pick out stitches when we make a mistake. It's appropriate." EV thought about pulling out her phone to key up the news and check if there had been a report on significant snowfall in hell—surely it must have just frozen solid.

Chloe's look of relief when EV stepped into the room said clearer than words how close they were to having the worst name in the history of knitting groups. "Knit Wits at least has a double entendre going for it. I like to think we're a witty group. Take Talia for instance." *Or just take her*, EV couldn't help thinking, "She's always ready with a quick word—Lottie, you've been the subject of many a sarcastic remark." Divide and conquer. For Talia and Lottie to get along more than ten minutes in a row might just set the world spinning backwards. Not that it would be a bad thing for general purposes, just not this one instance,

Sisters with only two years between them, Talia and Lottie looked nothing alike. Buxom Lottie flaunted her assets in closely fitted tops with plunging necklines paired with snug skirts or leggings. Coming or going, parts of her resembled two volleyballs battling for space in a pair of pantyhose. Talia, slightly younger and more circumspect than her older sister, had a body shaped more like the poles holding the net. Draped head-to-toe in unrelieved black, the widow weeds Talia wore almost daily since the loss of her husband Luther last summer did nothing for her figure.

"Knit Wits. I like the sound of it." Talia preened at the compliment without noticing its backhanded nature. "That's my vote."

"That's three for Knit Wits and one for Knitpickers." EV glanced over at Allegra Worth, who offered a shrug and the tiniest hint of a smirk. Her presence in the group remained a marvel to most. Allegra's recent history included an affair that resulted in the murder of her paramour, who just happened to be Talia Plunkett's brother-in-law. Holding her head high in a small town after that type of scandal took, in EV's estimation, a set of cast iron guts. Showing up to knitting group week after week proved she had a formidable set of something else as well. Yet, she declined to vote.

Still, with Jessamyn absent, that left only Priscilla's vote, which didn't matter anyway—EV had the majority. Priscilla's dark eyes glittered on either side of a veritable beak of a nose which, combined with her long neck and penchant for wearing hand knits in feathery yarns, gave her a distinctly bird-like appearance. Today, in downy white complete with... well, EV didn't quite know whether to call it a hat or a knit barrette—she was a dead ringer for a cockatoo.

"If I have to choose between the two, I'd go with Knitpickers. Knit Wits doesn't sound any more flattering than..."

Before she could finish, Allegra chimed in. "That's my vote, too. Now we have a tie."

"Then I say we table this for another week." Chloe's clacking needles spawned a steadily growing panel destined to be part of a cape-like garment with sleeves. Every straight and true stitch disgusted EV, who had been coming to knitting group for years, while this was only Chloe's fourth month. Drat the girl for being good at everything. Still, EV grinned with pride at the woman who was the closest thing to a daughter she would ever have. The grin widened when Chloe shot her a waggled eyebrow at dodging the naming bullet again.

"Shame about that accident on Elbow Hill last night. They say it's still touch and go for that Hawthorne woman. And did you hear? Christian hasn't left her side. Not even when her family came." Lottie would know, since two of her cousins worked at County General Hospital.

"She was just lucky he came along when he did. I think that boy spends half his time tromping through the woods." EV snatched her hands back when Priscilla not-so-gently pulled the needles—dripping with an uneven trail of pink—away to rescue several dropped stitches.

"Who attacked her?" Head tilted to the side, Lottie pinned EV with a look.

"How should I know?" EV replied.

"Oh, come on. You and your trusty sidekick over

there have your noses in it already. We're betting on you to solve the crime."

"Sidekick?" Chloe's left brow shot up.

"Partner in crime...no, wait, crime solving, then." Lottie waved off Chloe's one-word protest.

Talia's tone, when she chimed in, contained none of the sneer evident in her sister's, "You have to help that poor girl the way you helped me when I lost Luther and Evan. I don't know what I would have done if you hadn't..." she gave Allegra a sidelong glance to gauge her reaction to the topic. "...you just have to help her."

"We'll do what we can." And to change the topic, EV threw Chloe under the bus without the slightest hint of regret. "Did you and Detective Hottie set the date yet?" She actually felt the heat from Chloe's scorching glare.

"Not yet. Why rush things?"

And EV went for broke, "Dunno, thought you might be thinking about starting a family. You're not getting any younger, you know." There would be retaliation later, Chloe's look all but shouted that fact. EV didn't care. It was too much fun watching her squirm. Seeing Priscilla's eyes light up in the special way that meant she was seeing visions of a layette knitted from something fuzzy only added to EV's glee. Chloe would make a great mother, and the patter of little feet between the two homes would be welcome.

As though Chloe read her thoughts, "My place is too small for kids. Nate has to bend over to take a shower." She ignored the chorus of suggestive noises coming from the rest of the room, but Chloe's face tinted pink. "Speaking of kids, I wanted to talk to you all about Rhonda Erickson. She says she wants to keep working right up until the baby is born, but we've got WHaC coming up. Tank's projecting a big turnout and I can't see letting her waddle around on those tree trunk ankles, serving a bunch of college kids when she's already past her due date. EV and I were planning to take a few shifts, and I've tapped Mindy and Veronica as well. Can we count on the rest of you?"

"No!" Talia's unexpected exclamation surprised EV. "You two concentrate on helping Stacey Hawthorne. We'll cover The Mudbucket. Won't we, girls." She included Lottie and Allegra in a gimlet-eyed glare. "Can't have our best sleuths slinging hash when there's more important work to be done. Leave it in my capable hands, I'll work out a schedule. Now, tell us what you know about the accident."

Chloe steadfastly ignored the string of profanities uttered by Nate as she snuggled into bed between her two young cats, Sugar and Spice. Every evening, he vowed to remember to duck below the slanted ceiling and ill-placed linen cabinet while he brushed his teeth, and every evening he promptly forgot and bashed his head into one or the other.

"That's it. Tomorrow I'm making a supply list, and we're going to get started on the remodel as soon as the weather breaks. I know you love this house, but I cannot live the rest of my life hunched over, or I'm going to wind up with some serious back issues. It's like a frickin' doll house in here." When Nate stood at his full six-foot-two-inches and raised his arms, he could touch any ceiling in the place.

"My grandparents were both short, I don't know what to tell you!" Chloe shot back with mock indignation. She liked to give him a hard time, but relished the idea of them creating a comfortable home for themselves out of what her family had started over fifty years ago. One of the first things she had done after moving in was add a deck to the back of the house, navigating around the unevenness created by several stages of additions tacked on over the years. Nate understood Chloe's attachment to the place, and had already begun brainstorming ways to expand without altering the odd mix of cottage and southwestern styles that made up the front side of the house.

"What all are you thinking about remodeling, anyway?" Chloe asked, curious to see if their imaginations were running in the same direction.

Nate peered around for a moment before he answered. "Well, you've got this two-story section above the living room and bedroom, and the ceilings in these two rooms are still low, but not enough for me to feel like a hobbit. The foundation for the original, one-floor structure is sturdy enough that we could add a second level, raise the ceilings and add one more—or maybe even two more—bedrooms and another bathroom up there. You could move your office down here, and we could create a master suite and a nursery upstairs."

His eyes didn't quite meet hers as he spoke the last part, but joy swelled up in Chloe's throat and almost choked her. Launching herself off the bed and into his arms, she planted a long, lingering kiss square on his lips.

"So, you want to have babies with me, Mr. Harper? I like the sound of that." She murmured, nibbling his ear until he lost his train of thought.

"And how long do you think this whole process is going to take?" Chloe asked.

"Building with cordwood is time consuming, so I think it will take the whole summer. I can get a crew of volunteers together so we can save some money on that end. Horis, Tank, my dad, Dalton and EV, Franklin, and Jace. The wood and mortar are cheap, but running electrical and plumbing isn't, so that could throw a wrench in the works. But we're not even planning on getting married for at least a year, and it's not like you're going to want a big to-do of a wedding like your mother had...right?"

"Well, you know, I *did* have my heart set on the French Riviera, but..." she grinned as Nate blanched, then decided to let him off the hook. "Of course not, I want to get married here, in the fairy garden or down by the lake. Nothing crazy." Chloe realized now was the time to broach the subject of finances; one she had been putting off for several weeks.

"You know, we're not hurting for money..."

"What do you mean?"

"My mom set up a trust fund for me years ago.

When it matured, I started investing and lived off the money I made working odd jobs and writing on a freelance basis. At the time, I didn't really have a need for that much cash, and it was sort of fun to play around with it. Apparently, I inherited her knack for choosing stocks, because it's grown into a tidy sum. I've never cared that much about having lots of *things*, so I rarely touch it. Bottom line, neither of us will probably ever *need* to work if we don't want to."

Nate sat down on the bed, staring straight ahead as the realization of what Chloe was saying sunk in, but didn't open his mouth to speak.

"I never mentioned it before because people are weird about money, and I wasn't sure how you would react. Plus, I figured you must have some idea, what with Lila's obvious financial situation, and the fact that I'm not exactly a career woman. Writing a weekly column for a small-town newsletter doesn't pay the big bucks."

"Wow. I mean...wow. I've been stressing out about what I'm going to do after Dalton's fully trained to take over my post, and apparently the financial aspect doesn't even matter. I can't decide if that makes me happy, or makes me feel like less of a man."

Chloe slithered to the edge of the bed, ran her hands over his muscular shoulders, and snaked her arms around his waist. "I don't think you're less of a man; and actually, I respect the fact that you've created your own success. It's easy not to try as hard when you know you're not financially dependent on your salary. But this does mean that you can take your time deciding what you want out of your career, and what direction you want to go when you've finished with business here in the Pines. That's something to be happy about, so I hope you can find a way to enjoy it."

Nate's fingers raked through his hair, pulling it into adorably messy spikes. "Now I just have to figure out exactly what I want. It's not a position I'm familiar with; I've always had a clear path laid out in front of me. But these past few months—returning home, living this life with you—has made me realize it wasn't *my* path I was following."

"I'm sorry you're overwhelmed. I'm here for you. Whatever you need."

"I know." He clasped his arms around Chloe's waist, pulled her close, and deposited a kiss on the tip of her nose. "That's why I love you so much."

Chapter 6

Not merely a functional necessity, everyone also used Ponderosa Pines' town meetings as a prime opportunity for social interaction. As such, the tiny municipal building was always packed to the gills, and this occasion was no exception. The fact that a young woman had been attacked and nearly killed within feet of the town line a mere two days prior brought even the least civic-minded residents out of the woodwork. Had an entire table not been commandeered to hold the bevy of covered dishes earmarked for post-meeting consumption, the standing-room-only status would still have held. As it was, Chloe and EV shared a single seat, while Nate and Dalton stood in the back.

"I now call this quarterly meeting to order." Stirling Floyd spoke into the microphone, his voice dispelling all further conversation. Expectant silence followed while everyone in attendance eagerly waited to hear the official statement regarding Stacey's accident and attack. It wasn't exactly new information, seeing as how the gory details were already in wide circulation—thanks in no small part to Chloe and EV's unabashed snooping.

"We have a number of municipal matters to discuss, though I'm guessing by the increase in attendance that most of you are more interested in the crime that occurred on Monday evening. Let's lay the topic to rest, shall we? Nate Harper and Dalton Burnsoll are here to give a short statement." Stirling gestured for Nate and Dalton to take his place at the podium.

"You take point on this one." Nate whispered to his deputy's back. Soon, it would be Dalton's sole responsibility to address police-related issues, and now was as good a time as any for him to start.

Dalton responded with a squaring of his shoulders, and spoke with no trace of trepidation in his voice. "As many of you know, Stacey Hawthorne of Gilmore was involved in an accident out on route 15. Within a few minutes she was found and aided by one of our own—Christian West. In the meantime, she was approached and assaulted by a person or persons unknown. Her condition is still listed as critical."

"The time frame, and the fact that she was placed back in the vehicle rather than left in the snow suggests that Stacey was being followed, and that she may have known her attacker. If anyone has any information about Stacey—why she was willing to drive through a blizzard to get to town, whether she had any enemies—please contact me or Nate. Even the smallest detail could be of utmost importance, so don't hesitate."

"That's all the information we can give you at this time. No questions please, let's get on with the rest of the meeting."

Stirling reclaimed his place amid the chattering of an unsatisfied crowd. Ponderosa Pines, after all, was affectionately referred to as 'Busybody Central'; if you lived in town for any length of time, everybody not only knew your name, but your parent's names, your childhood nickname, and your most embarrassing moment. Personal privacy was a sought-after commodity, one in short supply, and then only tolerated when snooping couldn't uncover every morsel of truth to be obtained.

"Does anyone have new business to discuss?" Stirling asked, opening the floor.

Veronica, who had been on the edge of her seat all evening, raised a hand and was waved to the front of the room, pulling Mindy along beside her. EV shot a questioning glance toward Chloe, who shrugged. Whatever the two of them were up to, it was something they hadn't shared with her, which left Chloe feeling intensely interested, and at the same time, mildly offended. She focused on what they had to say.

"Hi everyone. You all know me, but if not I'm Veronica Stanwick. This is Mindy Hammond, and we are interested in opening a shop downtown."

Chloe's eyes widened in surprise; Veronica and Mindy had been talking about going into business together for years, but it had never seemed like anything more than a pipe dream. The sneaky wretches had never let on they were this close to actually pulling the trigger on a concrete plan.

"What we are proposing is a consignment shop with clothing and household items. I know that might sound counter-intuitive, given that we already have the co-op and that bartering is common around here—but we've noticed a steady increase in tourism over the past several years and believe the shop would do well if properly stocked. The primary purpose of the co-op is to handle the exchange and sale of meat and produce, but over time, other goods have started to overtake the space."

Mindy picked up where Veronica left off. "Let's face it, between knitting group and the sewing club, we're swimming in handmade items—many of which either don't get used or wind up being donated to charity. At our shop, a portion of the sale of any item you consign gets paid back to you in cash. Clothing and home decor items will be accepted, including handmade jewelry, art, or whatever you're looking to get rid of. We're not looking to replace the outlets where you are already selling your work, but to add to them. Right here in town, in a place where you can trust that you're getting paid for everything that sells." Being ripped off by vendors was the number one complaint among town artisans over the past year.

Knowing it would be a bone of contention, Mindy directed her next comments toward Willow and Rainn, owners of New Sage.

"We're not looking to compete with you, and we're willing to work closely with you to make sure that the gap we want to fill doesn't overlap and hurt your business." She widened her focus to include the rest of the assembly, "If you all agree, we would like to remodel the old schoolhouse, and use the main floor for the shop." Veronica contributed. "And Mindy has an idea for the second floor."

"Many of you attend my yoga classes each week; and those of you who do must realize that my living room is getting a little cramped. We were thinking we could turn the second floor into a studio, where I'll offer an expanded selection of classes—including that hot yoga one you've all been dying to try. I've been certified for it, but haven't wanted to live in a sauna." Mindy's grin was infectious, and already a number of people were smiling expectantly and offering signs of support.

Mindy moved aside so Stirling could take his place behind the podium once more to address the crowd. "The schoolhouse is municipal property, and as such is eligible for whatever use the town deems appropriate. Therefore, we must put the action to a vote. All in favor?"

With the bang of a gavel, ReStyled was born.

"It's the mob. You mark my words. I watch the news. I read the papers." Abe Zellner reminded EV of

Yosemite Sam when he got going. "I bet a Mafia Don put the clip on her for prosecuting one of his capo."

"The clip? Capo?"

"Clipped her." He scowled when she presented him with a blank stare. "A hit. Don't you know anything?"

I know you've been watching too much TV, EV mastered the intense desire to roll her eyes when he leaned in to whisper loudly, "I think she was on the lam and headed here to lie low until the heat died down." The man chewed garlic like a teenager chewed gum. Health benefits notwithstanding, EV thought his breath alone would send germs heading in the opposite direction with their disease-ridden tails between their legs. She blinked her watering eyes and tried to remember what he had just said.

"It's a theory."

"So go do something about it. For all we know there's a headhunter packing iron over in one of the inns."

Wishing someone—anyone—would come along and rescue her from this conversation, EV patted Mr. Zellner on the arm. A glance around the room proved she was on her own. Not a single eye turned in her direction—on purpose, no doubt. Rats, every single one of them.

"Excuse me, that's my phone."

"I didn't hear nothing."

"Vibrate." EV pretended to read a new text with some alarm. "It's important. I'll pass your concerns along, Abe." She made her escape while he moved on to expose his theory—and his withering breath—to another small knot of townspeople.

Glancing around the room again, EV noted the absence of several people who would normally have been on hand. David and Rhonda Erickson were missing, as were Tank Daniels and Jessamyn Sanders. Rhonda's due date had come and gone, leaving her with no baby and not a single shred of patience. During that time, customers watched poor David accept Rhonda's dire looks and recriminations for having gotten her into this mess with cheerful equanimity. Once the baby came, the uncomfortable, anxious, hormone-ridden woman would turn back into the sweet wife he had married. Tank and Jessamyn leaving early presented more of a mystery, given their usual presence among the after-meeting clean-up crew.

From across the room, Chloe flashed EV a rueful

smile. She'd been privy to at least five theories about Stacey's murder attempt. Her favorite was a joking speculation regarding a bad breakup after a torrid love affair with Horis who, upon hearing his name mentioned in that context, blushed a deep, brick red.

"For the love of Pete, I never even met the woman," he sputtered. "How did I get to be part of this?"

"It's because you're such a stud." Chloe teased. When she saw the stricken look on his face, she regretted the flip comment. A sweet man like Horis didn't deserve to be lonely. Not for the first time, Chloe resolved to do something to help him find someone. With that in mind, she quietly assessed his appearance. Under all that flannel, he carried plenty of muscle; getting him into a nice sweater and a pair of jeans that didn't come from the Farmer Ted section of Kmart might be a start. He wore bottle-bottom glasses over a drooping Fu Manchu mustache that pulled focus from warm, brown eyes and a chiseled chin. She'd bet the lips hiding under all that bristle would turn out to be full and inviting. A set of contacts and an hour in the barber's chair to tame his shaggy mane, and he'd be breaking hearts instead of clods of earth out in his fields.

Low benches flanked four long rows of handmade trestle tables lined up end to end down the length of the lower level of the meeting hall. Another table resting along the wall nearest the kitchen groaned under the weight of its potluck bounty. Chloe had her eye on an inch thick slice of steamed brown bread. Slathered with butter, the stuff tasted like heaven and rode the hips like double-dipped sin. Totally worth the extra thirty minutes of cardio; make that an hour, she decided when she saw there was both chocolate cream and peanut butter pie on the dessert end of the table.

Ahead of her in line, Nate selected a bit of this and a bit of that, but when he went for the mystery dish Priscilla always made, Chloe poked him in the back. "You're going to eat that?"

"Well, no one else took any, and I don't want her to feel bad. Besides, it could be good."

"It's gray." Chloe kept her voice low in case Priscilla was anywhere around.

"So?"

"Name another food that's gray. For that matter, name an ingredient that's gray. It could be meat, or it could be cake. No one knows, that's why they always stick it in the middle between the desserts and the entrees."

The more she protested, the more determined he became to eat some of whatever it was.

"What'll you give me if I finish it?"

"An antacid."

Nate rolled his eyes at her. "Give it a rest, Chlo. It can't be that bad."

"Don't say I didn't warn you." She followed him back to settle in beside Veronica, who sat directly across from Mindy, Jace, EV, and Dalton. A look at Nate's plate caused EV to raise an eyebrow.

"I told him," Chloe insisted. "He wouldn't listen."

Talk turned to Mindy and Veronica's newly-approved joint venture while everyone tucked in. Chloe noticed Nate saving his mystery dish for last.

Halfway through her brown bread, a comment from the bench directly behind her distracted Chloe from the conversation. Even with Dalton and EV finally becoming an item, the town cats had not sheathed their claws.

"Dalton would probably already have a suspect if Queen EV would climb up out of his pants long enough for him to think a little." Summer Daniels' venom-filled words carried clearly to Chloe's ears—

as did Millie Jacobs' braying twitter. Funny how Millie's laugh matched her horselike features so well, Chloe thought. Jealousy sat as poorly on the woman as the two-sizes-too-small sweater she wore. Cheapshot karma stilled Chloe's tongue, but at the cost of her blood pressure going up a notch or two. They weren't even trying to lower their voices.

EV's method of dealing with the pair of them tried Chloe's patience—in her opinion, a well-deserved blast trumped benign avoidance any day of the week, and twice on Sunday. A short but enjoyable fantasy involving a bucket of water and a smoking hiss as they dissolved like the witches they were played through Chloe's mind. Their husbands had always been safe from EV, who was not the type to poach, but you wouldn't know that from the way they acted.

It was more than the willowy body that refused to betray her over-fifty status; more than the angled face framed by a swing of sable hair, that attracted men to EV. Chloe thought it was the combination of polar opposites: confidence and vulnerability, that created a puzzle a man wanted to solve, and a lesser woman would find intimidating. Summer and Millie would always be among that group. Seeing that truth wasn't enough for Chloe to generate any sympathy for them.

Turning her attention back, she saw Nate pop the last gray bite into his mouth. "Animal, vegetable, or mineral?" She kept her voice low in case Priscilla was nearby.

"Yes." He tried to pull off nonchalant, but it didn't fly. Chloe observed him closely, looking for signs of indigestion.

"Which is it? Sweet or savory?" Her quiet demand was met with a smirk.

"You'll have to try some to find out for yourself." Manly pride on the line, he kept his opinion of the dish to himself. It wasn't easy. It's human instinct upon opening a jar of something gone bad, to take a whiff, make a face, and then offer to share the funk with a loved one. We've all done it.

"You've got a better chance of getting struck by lightning twice, with a winning lottery ticket in one hand, and a snowball in the other, while standing in the middle of hell, than of my taking a bite of that."

Nate grinned, "Then I guess you'll have to be happy with never knowing," and that was the last word she could pry out of him on the subject.

Chapter 7

"Initial reports just came in." Dalton poked his head around the doorway to the utility room where Nate was seated, cross-legged on the floor, organizing ancient case documents from the pre-computer age. The space, which could hardly be classified as a room at all, was so small both men couldn't comfortably fit inside at the same time. Fortunately, they were used to close quarters; tacked onto the back of the town's octagonal municipal building, their office used to house the entire collection of town records. Now they were crammed inside, forced to use an old broom closet as file storage.

"The breakdown on Stacey's attack? Excellent. I'll just get back to this...later." Nate yanked the door closed, knowing full well it would be days before any more filing got done, and took a seat at his desk. Not even to Chloe would Nate admit that the small office with the old-fashioned desks butted together, aligned facing each other, made him feel like he was a character in a film noir. The only thing missing was a natty brown suit, a skinny tie, and a fedora. "Lay it on me, what are we looking at?"

"According to the statement from her law partner, she was in the office on Monday, working a couple low priority cases. Nothing out of the ordinary. Office phone log says she got a call from Boston right before everyone clocked out early ahead of the storm." Business as usual for a Maine winter.

Scanning the sheaf of paper he had printed off, Dalton continued, "Missing briefcase—her law partner says she had it on her when she left—it hasn't turned up at her apartment, and he did mention she seemed a bit agitated about the weather."

Nate doodled something on a notepad he kept on his desk.

"Hair and fiber evidence will take a few days on the car, but they did find a sheet of paper stuck between the passenger side seat and door. Take a look."

Dalton passed Nate a photocopied document. "Does that say David Erickson?" Nate asked after perusing the page full of scribbled notes and doodles in Stacey's handwriting.

"Our very own. Shouldn't be difficult to find out what was going on there. Probably legitimate business; Rhonda's about to pop any second and they haven't owned the Mudbucket very long. Plus, he doesn't strike me as the crazy type, but then again, you never know. What else?"

"Here's something odd. There was no phone or laptop in her car. Now what kind of lawyer—or anyone, for that matter these days—doesn't carry a cell phone?" Dalton asked.

"He took them, the attacker. Probably the briefcase, too. She must have known something or had something on him that he didn't want anyone to find out. That's the most obvious theory."

"Which means there's probably way more to it than that." Dalton snorted. "Seems to be our luck."

"Your luck, soon enough." Nate sighed. "Though I might be able to assist in some capacity, since it looks like I'm facing life as an unemployed waste of space."

Dalton had no trouble pulling his eyes away from the case file at Nate's comment. "What's that supposed to mean?"

Nate shook his head. "Nothing, man, I'm just frustrated. Forget I said anything."

"Not happening. You're obviously going through something, and I need you on your game. We can have a real conversation without sacrificing our manhood. Now tell me what has you on edge."

"You know. I think EV's rubbing off on you." Nate's dry comment was tossed over his shoulder when he stood to pace the small room. "I think I'm having some kind of existential dilemma. When I got injured, I figured I'd take some time off, heal, and get right back to work. I didn't expect to come back to the Pines, though I'm not regretting that decision. If I hadn't, Chloe and I might never have reconnected, and I'd still be eating miserable takeout in my sad bachelor pad." He shook the image out of his head. Life before Chloe lacked meaning, color—it was a world bathed in shades of gray, and no job could ever come close to meaning as much to him as she did. He'd leave that mushy thought out of his narrative, though. "I thought I'd settled things job-wise, but now I'm getting blowback about my decision to stick around."

What Nate preferred to keep to himself was the conversation with his captain that basically laid it on the line: go back to Portland or stay in Ponderosa Pines, push Dalton out of a job, and lose the respect he had gained from his boss. Couched as a suggestion, Nate knew an ultimatum when he heard one. Out of sheer perversity, he wanted to choose option number three: walk away from the force and a job that no longer attracted him as it once had.

"Now, my choices are to live off my fiancée's trust fund—and compromise my manhood; commute to the city for work every day—and add hours to an already demanding schedule; or find myself a new career—which means taking a step back and starting over. I just don't know what the right answer is."

"Well, let me just say that sometimes, starting over can be a liberating experience." The *been there, done that* was implied. "I'm living proof you're never too old for change. Would Chloe consider moving to the city?"

Nate thought about that for a minute. "My gut says she would if I asked her to, but I won't. It would be like taking a flower out of a garden and planting it in a crack in the concrete. It would be pretty. And out of place. It's not just her, either. I've put down roots again. This is home."

Dalton tapped his pen against the scarred oak

desktop. "Can't hurt to at least look into your options; you never know, you might have missed your true calling. Something tells me Chloe will give you the space to make your own choices."

"I know. You're right. It'll work itself out, I guess." Nate returned to his desk chair and sat back, stroking his chin and appraising Dalton. "From here on out, though, you need to take ownership of this case. I have a feeling it will be my last, and it's your opportunity to prove you can handle things."

"Well, let's get it solved, then." He shot Nate an encouraging smile and flipped to the next page in the case file.

"Give me a summary; let me hear what you're thinking," Nate ordered.

"Okay, well, the victim, one Stacy Hawthorne, was coming down Route 15 at about 6:30—that's when Christian heard the crash. He got to her at 6:45. Within those fifteen minutes, a person unknown stopped, attacked Stacey, and took her briefcase, laptop, and phone before leaving the scene. We couldn't analyze the tire tread, thanks to contamination by the weather and rescue traffic. Christian reported seeing blood in the snow: CSU got a trace sample, but the lab reports it wasn't enough to run for DNA." Dalton rattled off.

"And the timeline?"

Dalton pulled his laptop toward him, "Victim left work at roughly 4:00 pm. We can place her at the Quickstop in Gilmore at 5:37 where she paid for gas with her debit card. Based on the distance and driving conditions, I'd say she had just about time enough to go home, change her clothes and pack a bag before heading out."

"Those are the facts—now tell me what you get from them."

"Well, I don't think it was random. I think he was following her, and maybe even drove her off the road. The guy—and I'm assuming it was a man—stole her files, her phone, and her laptop—but only rifled through the overnight bag containing personal items. He was looking for something, and I'm guessing when she didn't give it up, he got violent. If Stacey wakes up, she can tell us more. But that's a big if— she suffered a serious head injury, and the chances of survival aren't great. If she dies, it's first-degree murder."

Nate's brow furrowed at Dalton's last remark.

"Are you forgetting the bruising on her throat? He choked her. What does that tell you?"

"He wasn't cold or clinical—she made him mad."

"Right," Nate nodded. "He got up close and personal."

"Well, one thing I've learned—90% of this job consists of looking for needles in haystacks. Let's see what we can learn about her case load. Maybe something will stick out."

"I'll make the call; it'll probably be a day or two before we get anything back, but that gives us time to investigate a little closer to home."

"Sounds like a plan."The first house ever built in Ponderosa Pines, EV's place had been added onto more than once—no small feat considering the nature of alternative home building. Solid walls built from stacked cordwood in a matrix of mortar were meant to last several lifetimes, but adding doors and windows to them after the fact was difficult to impossible. To that end, EV's parents had chosen to build a post and beam framework with four-foot sections of log wall between the upright posts. When it came time to extend the home, any section of logs could be removed to create an access point between the new and the old.

Before dinner, Nate wandered around to assess how each new section had been joined to the old. If he and Chloe were going to be doing something similar next summer, he wanted to be prepared. EV gave him the album of photos she had taken during each phase, and he got lost in those for a while.

Still, tension filled the air all through another shared dinner that night. The two men talked about everything from sports to the weather, while EV remained stoic, accepting compliments on her vegetable stew and homemade peasant bread as if her mind remained empty of the hundred questions running rampant there. Chloe, on the other hand, maintained an irritated expression until dessert was presented, and then she finally snapped.

"You're really going to make us beg for information? Come on, you two. What did you find out?" Chloe practically screamed.

Nate turned to meet her gaze in exaggerated slow motion, enjoying the pulsating vein threatening to burst at her temple. "What do you think, Deputy?" he directed at Dalton. "Should we fill them in, or start a pool on how long it will take them to ferret out the facts on their own?"

Dalton, who would have chosen the shortest time

possible in such a pool, quirked a smile at him. They'd already decided what to share with the women—drawing out the tension over dinner had been payback for the worry caused by their excursion through the blizzard the other night.

"Stacey's work files, laptop, and phone are all missing. Everyone in her law office is being as cooperative as they can without breaking attorney/client privilege. The only lead we have is that she was coming to town to meet with a client. *We* will be checking up on it first thing in the morning."

"Who's the lead?" EV asked, speculation evident in the gleam of her eye.

"Why do you want to know?" Dalton challenged.

"We just want to help." Chloe supplied simply. "People talk to us; they let things slip. If someone in town knows why this happened to Stacey, we might be able to help you catch him sooner rather than later."

Nate sighed, "I know you want to use your uncanny ability to pry for all the right reasons, but realistically, nothing we've learned points a finger toward anyone in town. Whoever did this was behind her on the road. It could be a case of random violence. A woman driving alone during poor weather can easily become a target for certain types of crime."

"Sexual assault." EV filled in the blank. "It could explain why he choked her."

"We can't rule it out given the circumstances, but there's no real evidence to support that theory. Right now, we're looking for something a little closer to home." Dalton saw the same dismay mirrored on Chloe and EV's faces. "I didn't mean we're looking at anyone local as a person of interest, but we're sifting through Stacey's past for anyone who might have held a grudge."

"And hopefully, you're right. But while you're focusing on outside forces, we can see what kind of skeletons are in Stacey's closet. It might be impor-tant." EV gave Nate her best steely gaze—the one she used on misbehaving children—while Chloe went with her best Bambi eyes.

"It's David and Rhonda Erickson." Nate finally relented, knowing they would find out regardless of how many roadblocks placed in front of them, but refusing to relay every detail of the case file. "But you really do need to leave this to us. I am a trained detective, you know. It isn't like I've never had to question a witness or a suspect before."

"No one doubts your detective skills, Nathaniel." EV rolled her eyes. "We are merely suggesting that certain people are more likely to open up to someone they see as non-threatening as opposed to a cop looking for answers."

"Care to bet money on that fact?" Dalton contributed, a glint in his eye.

"Don't encourage them! Every time they get involved with something, they nearly get themselves killed. You're not helping!"

"I'll take that bet! A hundred bucks says we have more info by tomorrow night than you do." Chloe reached over the table to shake Dalton's hand on it, ignoring the steam blasting out of Nate's ears.

"Maybe you're not ready to take over," Nate accused Dalton, "if you're going to fold like a cheap suit every time one of them bats an eye at you." He ignored a second round of EV's stink eye when it fell on him.

"Hey, man, what can it hurt? If they find something we can use, excellent. If not, no harm done." Dalton nodded toward EV, "I'll guarantee her texting app has been getting a workout all day, and that one," he pointed a thumb toward Chloe, "has been mining the tip line for nuggets of info."

Chloe gasped, then turned on EV, "You told him?"

"It wasn't me." EV held up both hands in a gesture of innocence.

"Don't even look at me for this. I haven't said a word to him about it." Nate jumped in before she could accuse him.

"No one told me, Miss Babble and Spin." He leaned back in his chair with a self-satisfied grin. "What? You thought I didn't learn any detecting skills until this one came along?" A nod of his head indicated Nate. "I can see I've been grossly underesti-mated." Dimples flanked a wide grin below twinkling brown eyes.

"How did you figure it out?" Narrow-eyed, Chloe wasn't worried that he would tell anyone, she just wanted to know what had given her away.

"You have your methods, I have mine." And that was the last Dalton would say on the subject. Turning back to Nate, he said, "They're going to pry anyway, might as well give in gracefully."

Nate accepted defeat, knowing that more protesting would only encourage his fiancée and her friend to up the ante. "Fine, but this is on you, Deputy, if they get into trouble."

"Then it's settled." Dalton turned his attention toward the women. "But please be discreet. You don't need to go making yourselves targets again."

"Hah!" Nate huffed. "That'll be the day."

Chapter 8

"Quick, here they come." Chloe practically shoved EV through the door of New Sage. Next door to The Mudbucket and flanked by Thread on its other side, the store was packed to the gills with an eclectic mix of items. High-end pots and pans shared shelf space with chicken feed and home-opathic remedies. The scent of exotic spices that wouldn't grow locally blended with the smell of hay, imported coffee beans, and beeswax candles. Every time she walked through the door, Chloe stopped and sighed with delight at the heady aroma. Today, though, she and EV both almost tripped over a bag of sow chow in their hurry to get out of sight before Nate and Dalton could catch them trying to get to Rhonda and David Erickson first.

Willow, the male half of the crunchy, granola couple who owned New Sage, quickly apologized and shouldered the fifty-pound bag as though it weighed nothing. "I was in the middle of rearranging some things and forgot I'd left this here." Chloe would have bet Willow started life with a name like Ira Rosenstein, given the shape of his profile, while his wife, Rainn, was a local girl maybe fifteen years younger than EV. The eldest of ten children in the Thompson clan, Rainn had been joined with Willow in a handfasting ceremony during Chloe's first year back. Ripely pregnant with their third child, Rainn's vows had included a diatribe on the notion of owner-ship in marriage before announcing that as of this moment forward, she and Willow had chosen to be known by first names only in order to avoid any misconceptions. They'd tied the knot—literally—and she'd promptly gone into labor.

"No worries, Willow. We're fine." Since they were there, EV checked with Rainn to see if the shipment of Good Earth tea had come in yet. Their Sweet and Spicy blend was almost an addiction for her.

Headed toward the far-right corner at the back of the store, Chloe figured she would kill two birds and replenish her supply of unfiltered vinegar. Ever since trying a recipe for fresh sour pickles using her vacuum sealer, she had been going through the stuff like water. Bottle in hand, she turned back toward the register to see a man standing in the boxed goods section. He held a bag of moose-shaped novelty pasta in his hand, but his attention was focused on EV's conversation with Rainn.

"Busy this week?" EV expected nothing less given the student invasion during SHaC, the summer version of the conference, earlier in the year.

"Been run off my feet. I feel sorry for that poor Erickson girl. Bet she had no idea when they left the city for some peace and quiet that she'd end up slinging coffee for a bunch of college kids." Rainn's voice carried clearly throughout the store.

As Chloe watched, the man's chin lifted, he turned his ear toward the conversation, and his body stilled. Nothing Rainn said should have triggered such intense focus. Maybe he was having indigestion. Shrugging off the vague feeling of uneasiness, Chloe took her vinegar to the counter, paid for it, then leaned in and with a conspiratorial smile, whispered to Rainn, "Mind if we slide out the back door?"

"Avoiding Lottie again?" A little eyebrow waggle mislead without a bold-faced lie. "Sure, go ahead."

. . .

Nate and Dalton walked into the Mudbucket, jaws set with determination. They weren't about to be shown up by Chloe and EV again on the information-gathering front. David Erickson had made contact with Stacey not long before her attack, and since it was the only reference to Ponderosa Pines found amongst her belongings, both men hoped he would know something useful.

"Hi, David. We know you're busy, but if we could take a moment of your time to ask a few questions regarding Stacey Hawthorne." Dalton's statement was worded as if the man had a choice, but his tone indicated nothing less than full cooperation would be tolerated. Nate observed the exchange with pride. Dalton's demeanor had changed in the last few weeks—self-assurance and authority oozed out of his pores.

"Grab yourselves a cup of coffee and have a seat. I'll be right over as soon as I get a chance." He looked around the room once and back at Nate and Dalton apologetically. As thankful as he was for the extra help, Talia and her bevy of drafted workers hadn't been able to fall into the routines he and Rhonda had perfected over the last year. It would take weeks to put the kitchen to rights and find all the items no longer in their customary places. Ten minutes passed while the detective and deputy watched as he bustled around the cafe that had once belonged to Dalton and his ex-wife Marlene.

"How weird is it to come in here and see someone else running the place?" Nate prodded gently. It was common knowledge that Dalton's wife had left him for another woman, but even Nate didn't bring up the topic unless it was absolutely necessary.

A nostalgic smile crossed Dalton's lips. "Now, it's easy—a relief, even. Right after Marlene left it was harder. I don't hold it against her, don't get me wrong. We had a lot of good years together, and we loved each other a lot. But she had to forge her own path, and now I get to forge mine. Plus, if I had to be covered in donut glaze for another day of my life, I was going to snap."

"I hear that. Sometimes, back in Portland when I had a really heavy case load, it started to seem like the entire world was going to hell. Violent crimes weren't prevalent; Portland's a pretty safe city. But people still lie, cheat, steal, abuse children—those things happen everywhere. I'm beginning to think a life change would be good for me, too."

Any advice Dalton wanted to give had to wait as David finally emerged from the back of the cafe and took a seat at their table.

"How can I help you?" he asked.

"Sorry to interrupt, David. Just a few questions. First, how well did you know Stacey?"

"Not very, I'm afraid. She worked with us on the grant application for this place, and then her partner handled the title and closing. I hadn't spoken to her since, until about a month ago when we asked if she could help us draw up a will before the baby comes. Rhonda thought we might get too busy afterward and forget all about it, so I agreed to handle it all now." David's soft smile spoke volumes about what he would do to placate his uncomfortably pregnant wife. "Stacey faxed us some forms to fill out with our information and mail back to her."

"And when were you planning on meeting with Stacey? Did you make an appointment?" Nate interjected.

"A couple weeks from now, I think. But she called the day of her accident and said she had everything ready to sign. You don't think that's why she was out driving, do you?" David asked with wide eyes, as if the idea had just occurred to him.

"We have no reason to think so at this time, but it's possible. Is there anything else you can tell us?" Nate fixed him with his bad-cop stare, but David appeared nonplussed by it.

"Nothing I can think of. I know where to find you if I do."

EV ducked low in the passenger's seat of Chloe's Mini Cooper, where they'd taken refuge after exiting New Sage. Long, cold minutes passed before Nate and Dalton left the Mudbucket and headed back to their office around the corner.

"I see you found a use for my sunglasses and scarf." Chloe teased, her eyes raking over EV's outfit.

EV stuck her nose in the air and avoided Chloe's gaze, but removed the offending items and tucked them into the glove compartment. "I was trying for Meryl Streep, and was totally pulling it off, so bite me."

"Well, I don't think they spotted us, though they probably knew we'd be trailing them. We'd better get this show on the road if we're going to make any headway before tonight."

The day having dawned bright and clear for the first time in nearly a week, the streets were alive with Piniacs running errands, socializing, and stocking back up on supplies in case the good fortune wasn't destined to hold. Of course, each and every resident seemed in need of a caffeine jolt, and the Mudbucket was filling up quickly. David Erickson didn't notice their entrance specifically, so Chloe and EV hung back, awaiting a place in the queue.

Horis Wentworth's voice pitched over the din of the group crowded around the counter, "...take it in stride. This is a safe place, despite the attack. And the murder we had here a few months ago."

"Murder, really? Guess bad things happen everywhere. Still, in this sleepy little town? What happened?" Chloe recognized the tall, handsome stranger as the man she had seen listening in on EV and Rainn next door, and leaned around a cluster of other waiting customers for a better look. Out of the corner of her eye, she saw EV doing the same.

"Never seen him before. Which is really too bad." EV whispered under her breath, taking in his long, lean frame and sexy, full-lipped grin.

"You ain't kidding." Chloe's left eyebrow raised a fraction of an inch while she let out a low whistle.

"And now let's never speak of it again." She winked at EV, who nodded in agreement though, in truth, Chloe wasn't feeling him. After Detective Hottie, any man would pale in comparison. It gave her a little tingle just thinking about Nate and the way his mouth fitted so perfectly against her own.

"Go talk to Horis. Find out who he is and why he's asking so many questions. I'm going to give David a hand; he's in over his head." EV pushed Chloe toward the burly man. Horis' status as a close, personal friend made any objection Chloe may have had null and void, so she sidled up to him and trained her eyes on the newcomer expectantly.

"Hey Chloe, how's it going?" Horis slung an arm around Chloe's shoulders and squeezed her into his usual quick hug. "Have you met Chet Morgan? He's in town to cover WHaC for a regional magazine and thinks Ponderosa Pines is a little on the odd side."

"Nice to meet you, Chet. And we prefer the term "eccentric", if you don't mind." Her light tone took all reproach from the comment.

"Whatever you say." Chet looked Chloe up and down, drinking in her trim, taught frame appreciatively. Before indignation could solidify and leak out of her mouth, he bid them all goodbye and turned to exit the cafe. More than one female head followed his progress from the room, and a spate of giggles erupted from the table where Talia and Lottie enjoyed their breakfast sandwiches.

EV, handing a pair of lattes over the counter, loosed a ladylike snort. "Yeah, that's going to be a problem if Nate ever sees him giving you the googly eye."

"I don't like him. What an arrogant jerk. And why is he nosing around asking questions?"

"Relax, he's not the first visitor to wonder about our town. It happens all the time."

Chloe's lower lip jutted into a pout. "Well, he's on my list anyway." EV could only pity the poor guy; Chloe's list wasn't a place she'd put her own worst enemy.

David finally greeted them after dropping coffee and a couple of bear claws off at a table near the door. "Thanks for the help, EV. You're a lifesaver. You just missed Nate and Dalton. They were headed back to the office."

"Actually, we came to see Rhonda. Is she upstairs?" EV asked hopefully.

"She sure is, go on up."

EV led Chloe through the kitchen, then up a flight of stairs to a landing with a small storage area lined with shelves stacked high with boxes of to-go cups, coffee filters, and packets of sweetener. A sharp left turn took them into a short hallway that opened into the small studio apartment where Rhonda lounged on an old, comfortable-looking couch, sipping a cup of herbal tea.

"Hey there, can we come visit with you for a bit?" EV knocked on the wall lightly, startling Rhonda, who hadn't noticed their approach.

"Oh, jeez, you surprised me! Sure, come on in. Have a seat."

"I didn't know there was an apartment up here." Chloe looked around the room appraisingly. "It's really cozy."

"Dalton's daughter spent summers here during college. Now it's just an escape for us when things are slow or it's too crazy to go all the way home. If we have a super early delivery, we sometimes stay over to save that extra half hour of sleep. It's going to be a lifesaver when the baby comes."

"Can't be much longer, right?" EV eyed Rhonda's

swollen belly and silently counted back through the last few months.

"My due date was two weeks ago. Doc Talbot says first babies are often late, but it needs to happen soon because I'm out of room in there, and he's been tap dancing on my bladder for the past few days. So, what did you ladies trudge all the way up here to talk to me about?" It was Rhonda's turn to eye the two of them with a twinkle of amusement in her bright blue eyes.

"We wanted to ask you about Stacey Hawthorne."

"Oh, well, that's not what I was expecting. Were you friends with her?" She looked from Chloe to EV and back again. EV must have known Stacey, Rhonda thought, since she'd been the one to help with the grant paperwork for The Mudbucket.

"No, not exactly." Chloe began. "We just want to help figure out who did this to her."

EV cut in. "Truth be told, we were sort of forced into the investigation. If we want to continue to be welcomed at knitting group, we've at least got to make an attempt." At Rhonda's puzzled expression EV elaborated. "The ladies who knit seem to think that because we figured out who killed Evan Plunkett and solved the Yeti crisis, we're equipped to solve every mystery in a 100-mile radius. Stacey didn't deserve to be assaulted, so it doesn't feel right for us not to try to help if we can."

Rhonda seemed satisfied and agreed to answer any questions she could. "Unfortunately, I don't know anything at all about her personal life, so I'm not sure I'll be much use. What would you like to know?"

"When was the last time you talked to her?"

Rhonda repeated the same story David had given to Nate and Dalton half an hour before, adding that she had been the one to answer the phone when Stacey called.

"We had asked her to put together a will for us to sign. I wanted to get it out of the way before the baby came. David told her what we wanted, and we filled out all the paperwork and mailed it back to her. That was a few weeks ago and we weren't expecting to hear back from her so quickly."

"When you talked to her on the phone, did she say she was planning to stay in town for the duration?"

"No. Why?"

"There was an overnight bag in her car, she'd packed enough clothes for a few nights away." EV hated to give away any privileged information, but there didn't seem to be any way around it.

"Maybe she figured if she couldn't beat the snow, she'd just hole up here and wait out the storm."

"That might be it." Chloe wasn't convinced.

"All she said was that she was going to head out before the storm hit, and that she'd drop off the paperwork then. Maybe she had other business in town. I did give Tank Daniels her card a few weeks ago. He mentioned needing some legal advice, so I told him about Stacey. It's a long shot, but maybe you should talk to him."

"Thanks, Rhonda. Anything else that you can think of?"

"Now you mention it, she seemed brusque on the phone. Not quite herself. She didn't ask how I was doing, or how the baby was doing, and it struck me as odd. In the past she's always been very friendly—and it wasn't that she was unfriendly exactly; it was more like she was distracted and tense. I wasn't offended; I figured she was busy. But I did notice the difference from our earlier conversations."

. . .

As manager of the co-op, Tank spent a fair amount of time updating paperwork, so when Chloe and EV didn't find him there, they doubled back to where his farm sat across from Abe Zellner's place on the northwest edge of town. Tank's girlfriend, Jessamyn Sanders peeked through a curtain covering the windowed door before opening it and inviting them inside.

Something of an enigma, Jessamyn was one of Ponderosa Pines' newest inhabitants. One day she had rolled into town on her motorcycle—no more than the basic necessities in her saddlebags—spent a weekend camping out in one of the public areas, and the next Monday, rented a furnished apartment in the newest section of town. It didn't appear that she worked for a living, having spent every sunny summer day lounging by the community pool. However, Chloe happened to know that she did free-lance data entry for a national company—one best known for their top-of-the-line accounting software, but that also offered home loans and full-service bookkeeping.

"Tank's in the living room. Follow me." She led them through a well-stocked kitchen: open shelves contained stacks of pots and pans in every imaginable shape and size; mugs and teacups hung from a large pegboard backsplash positioned behind a complicated-looking espresso machine; and an impressive collection of herbs and spices in carefully-labeled jars filled a floor-to-ceiling wire rack. Apparently, Tank was also handy in the kitchen, though you'd never know it by looking at him. The restaurant quality range with its six huge burners confirmed the futility of judging a man by his cover-alls—a common theme in town, since Ponderosa Pines seemed to draw people with uncommon histories and interests. In addition to being a confirmed foodie, Tank was also an MIT-trained engineer specializing in alternative energy, who had traveled all over the world to work with the very best in his field before ending up on a farm in the middle of nowhere.

"Hi, Tank, do you have a few minutes to talk to us?" EV greeted him brightly. The two were on good terms, EV having logged more than a few shifts at the co-op herself.

"Of course, anything for you, EV." His wide blue eyes crinkled at the corners when he grinned, which was much more frequent since he and Jessamyn began dating. "I'm just putting the finishing touches on my opening lecture, then I'm headed back over to finish setting up. We could use some more volunteers if you ladies aren't busy." He cajoled.

"We're both signed up for shifts tomorrow afternoon." EV assured him. "We were hoping you might be able to tell us something about Stacey Hawthorne. It's a shame what happened, and you know how we like to…ahem…get involved in community issues."

Jessamyn looked up from the box of teaching materials she was packing at the mention of Stacey's name, her face pale as she waited for Tank's response.

"It *is* a tragedy. I don't know her very well, but she has been helping me negotiate with my former employer for the rights to that cooling system I designed last year. She was…" he stopped himself, "…is an excellent negotiator. I hope she pulls through."

Jessamyn leaned forward, elbows resting on her knees "Is there any word on her condition? Was she just in the wrong place at the wrong time, or was the attack premeditated? I know your fiancée is on the case, Chloe, do you know if they have a lead yet?" The urgency in her voice struck EV as a bit strange.

"Did you know Stacey?" EV gentled her voice.

"I thought I would be safe here." Jessamyn didn't

actually answer the question, nor did her eyes lift to meet EV's. She lurched to her feet, "I've got to..." She hurried from the room.

"She's concerned." Tank covered for her. "We all should be." His worried glance strayed in the direction where Jessamyn had gone. His need to follow and soothe his girlfriend was palpable.

"All right, it's time to compare notes. Hope you have a nice, crisp Benjamin Franklin ready." Chloe addressed Dalton as she walked through the door of the office behind the municipal building with EV following at a more sedate pace. Nate's withering look did nothing to put a damper on Chloe's buoyant mood, which became even lighter as she caught the half-smile Dalton shot her behind Nate's back.

EV squeezed in around Chloe, deposited a kiss on Dalton's cheek, and took one of the two small chairs crammed into a space below the only window in the building. Chloe followed suit, and looked up at Nate expectantly.

"I don't see how you could have come up with any more than we did. David Erickson was a dead end." Nate declared, though his confidence dipped with every passing second as Chloe's grin widened.

EV raised her right eyebrow, stated simply. "And that's why you should have tried talking to Rhonda instead", and gestured for Chloe to explain.

"Rhonda spoke to Stacey on the day of her accident. David had called the office about putting together a will, but it was Rhonda who handled the details." Nate's eyes narrowed, but he didn't interrupt, so she continued. "When she called, Stacey told Rhonda she was planning on getting here before the storm got bad. When Stacey didn't show, Rhonda assumed she had come to her senses and decided to wait."

"Did Rhonda have any idea if Stacey planned to meet with anyone else?"

"No, not exactly. Rhonda said she gave Stacey's card to Tank Daniels a few weeks back. Stacey was negotiating a deal over a set of engineering plans he was selling to a big corporation, but it was pretty cut and dried and he had no plans to see her anytime soon."

Nate's right leg bobbed up and down; Chloe could hear his knee lightly bumping the underside of the desk, and knew that if they weren't packed into the room like a can of sardines he'd be pacing around anxiously. "You're saying you don't actually know any more than we do, or am I missing something?" he asked.

"That's not entirely correct. Rhonda mentioned that Stacey wasn't herself; she was not as friendly as she usually is, and she seemed distracted. That's something. Oh, and Tank seemed on the up-and-up, but Jessamyn was there and she seemed a little too amped for someone who doesn't even know the victim."

EV cut in. "She looked like she'd recently stopped crying; puffy eyes, red nose. Maybe she and Tank had a fight, or she's getting a cold; I don't know. But it's a line to tug, anyway."

"Jessamyn doesn't seem a likely suspect. For all her combat boots and bravado, she's not much of a badass." Dalton mused before noticing the quizzical expression on EV's face and continuing, "She likes to fish down at the pond, and I spend a lot of time there in the summer. We've talked a few times, and she seems like a nice, down-to-earth woman who's going through a life change. Not a hit-someone-on-the-head-and-leave-them-for-dead kind of person."

"We don't necessarily think she's the attacker; but maybe she knows something."

Nate, though he hated when they meddled—mostly out of protectiveness—was secretly impressed. "We'll look into it. I'd say thank you, but it'll just go to your heads."

"So, where's our hundred bucks?" Chloe held out her hand.

"Don't push your luck." Nate kissed Chloe with an indulgent smile that rubbed her the wrong way.

"A bet's a bet."

"Talk to Dalton, he's the one who shook on it. It's not my deal." Nate tossed his partner to the wolves with nary a second thought.

EV rounded on Dalton, "He's right. Pay up."

"Double or nothing?" Dalton leaned past EV to issue the challenge to Chloe.

"Fine, but this time, it's not just money. We win, you walk down Main Street in women's clothes."

Not even missing a beat, Dalton countered, "When we win, you'll organize the filing room."

Nose in the air, Chloe shook on it.

"I'll be looking forward to giving up that job," Nate kissed Chloe on the nose, and ushered her and EV out the door. "I'll be home soon. Love you."

Chapter 9

Waking up from a dream where a chicken with Priscilla's head squawked and pecked at the ground while Lottie, Sabra, and Talia wrestled in a nearby pigpen unnerved EV so badly she settled for caffeine-free herbal tea instead of coffee. No stimulants or spicy food for a day, and maybe a gallon of brain bleach would be enough to clear it out of her head. Or two of them. If she'd had any idea how mildly prophetic that dream was about to become, she would have ordered a truckload.

Instead, she turned to chores to help wipe the images from her mind. The kitchen floor could use a good hands-and-knees scrubbing.

Four texts hitting EV's inbox at the same time unleashed a muttered curse on the genius who invented texting. Life was so much easier when she could leave the house and the phone behind. These days, if she didn't answer a text within fifteen minutes, it was assumed she must be lying somewhere dead or dying, and a flurry of texts would be issued to Chloe and/or Dalton urging them to go check on her. It was the next best thing to being chipped like a dog. Worse, it made her feel like one of those old ladies from the clapper commercial. Did they think she had fallen and couldn't get up?

Giving in, EV wrenched off a pair of hot pink rubber gloves, tossed the sponge into murky water, and took a look at the screen

Sabra and Lottie are at it again. -Priscilla

World War Three at the B&Bs. -Allegra

Come quick. -Talia

Stuck in Gilmore. Multiple reports. Sabra. Lottie. Can you deal? XX -Dalton

As she was reading, the text noise sounded again.

I'm at Lottie's. -Talia

Thumbs flying, EV typed one of her own.

Pick you up in ten. Got any popcorn? Battling innkeepers. She sent the text winging off to Chloe, dumped the bucket of dirty water, and sighed over the still-dirty half a floor that wouldn't be finished today. Well ahead of the ten-minute time frame, Chloe popped through the kitchen door.

"No popcorn. I've got pretzels, though. Any idea what it's all about?"

"Guest poaching as usual, I'd assume. I say we ought to let them duke it out."

"Who would you bet on to win?"

"Sabra." EV answered quickly.

"Really? Lottie's meaner...and bigger."

"Sabra is quietly stubborn. She's like the Energizer Bunny."

"I'm driving. It'll take half an hour to get there in that heap of yours. Coop's already warmed up."

EV grumbled a little but gave in. Her ancient pickup was dependable, but for short hops to town it required fifteen minutes of idling in the driveway in order to get it to throw heat by the time she arrived at her destination. Chloe's battered Mini Cooper felt like it heated up faster, if only because riding with her behind the wheel raised EV's blood pressure. There was a reason the car looked twice its age.

Riding through town, EV wondered if Mother Nature had gone a bit senile this year. After a relatively light winter, having two feet of powdery white stuff on the ground at this point felt all kinds of wrong. Tall banks lined both sides of the road into town, where everything seemed quiet considering the spate of new arrivals due in before Tank's opening lecture at the co-op this evening.

Whatever was going on at the end of Altamont Lane hadn't reached this far yet. A left at the edge of town took them past End Road, where Tank Daniels and Abe Zellner owned adjacent farms. A trail just barely accessible by tractor or truck in summer, and used for snowmobiles in the winter ran down the line behind Zellner's place where it bordered Lottie Calabrese's parcel of land. That same trail wound around and through the woods to become part of the network of riding and walking paths connecting the entire town.

Slowing now, Chloe prepared to turn right onto Altamont when a pair of signs jammed into the snowbank on either side of the road came into view.

Come On Inn blazed in red lettering above the words Best Breakfast in Town in black.

On the other side of the road EV saw Open House —also in red—with the tagline: Sleep in Comfort and Style.

"And there it is," EV commented dryly.

"It gets worse," Chloe nodded to indicate a line of smaller signs lining the road. Driving slowly, she read out the ones on Lottie's side while EV quoted the rest.

On Sabra's side of the road the signs read: Pie to Die for; Free Lunch, And Dinner, Beds like Clouds.

Chloe read out: Upscale Comforts, Private Bathrooms, Relaxing Atmosphere, Stay 2 nights, Get 1 Free.

"Looks like this escalated quickly." There was no time for Chloe to elaborate on that thought when she turned the last corner and had to jam on the brakes. Several cars filled the driveways, indicating both inns were running at close to full capacity. From their vantage point, EV and Chloe saw Lottie and Sabra squaring off in the middle of the road. Without even bothering to pull over, Chloe jammed the car into park and the two of them hurried toward the scene.

"My beds are just as comfortable as yours, Sabra Pruitt, and my guests sleep on Egyptian cotton."

"Are you saying my sheets don't measure up to yours?"

"Well, if the thread count fits..." Lottie practically spit the words out.

Guests, most wearing puffy parka coats, watched the show from both front porches.

"...I have every right to advertise the finer points of my establishment," Lottie continued.

"Advertising is one thing; luring my lodgers away with free nights is something else entirely."

"How is that different from offering them free food? That pie cost me a family of four."

Sabra sneered, "Your taste for touch-me-not white decor cost you that reservation. Parents can't relax when they have to make sure their kids aren't touching anything all the time."

"Oh yeah? Well, touch this," Lottie reached down to scoop a handful of snow and shove it in Sabra's face. The crowd on her porch cheered. To them, this was a fun bit of dinner theater.

Caught between wanting to watch it all play out and having given her word to put a stop to the fight, EV stepped into the fray just in time to catch a faceful of Sabra's retaliation.

"That's enough." EV's snow-covered glare touched on Chloe, who heaved with silent laughter from the sidelines, but was mostly pointed at the two women with chests heaving and eyes still spitting fury at each other.

As though she'd just been snapped out of a trance, Lottie's gaze fell on EV with a double-take. She turned her head slowly toward where a sea of faces watched with expressions ranging from amusement to mild astonishment from her own porch. Leaning sideways for a better view, Lottie saw the exact same mix reflected back at her from Sabra's porch.

What had gotten into the two of them to act this way in front of paying customers? And worse, in front of her newest arrival, the handsome and mysterious Chet Morgan.

He'd blown in with the storm the other night, waking her from a sound sleep with an insistent knock. She remembered the confused look on his face when she'd asked if he was with the tour, but he'd confirmed it by picking up a flier from her check-in counter.

"You mean this tour? Sure. I'm covering it for EcoPress." At her blank look, he elaborated. "You won't have heard of us. We only print quarterly, and our distribution is local." His voice, rough and deep, with a hint of Ireland running through, sent a shiver up her spine. In Lottie's head, a video played on fast forward. By the end of the week, he would profess his love for her, and whisk her off to meet his beloved Grannie in the land of the green. A white wedding dress, a new home, and, to still the ticking of her biological clock, a baby swaddled in blue. Forty wasn't too old to start a small family. Women were having babies at fifty these days.

His handsome looks made her breathless. The square chin and a nose that could have been chiseled from marble played nicely off eyes the gray of a winter sky. His hair, darkened by time to a coppery brown, had probably started out as strawberry blond if the masculine scruff on his cheeks was anything to judge by. He'd do—and with a good woman behind him, he'd soon find a more worthy venue for his talents.

A rush of heat flamed Lottie's face to a mottled red.

"I'm sorry, Sabra," the words emerged from gritted teeth. This fight, same as every other, had less to do with business rivalry than it did with personal history. If this winter version of tours went like the spring ones had, both of them would be turning away paying customers by the end of the day, anyway. Unless this fight emptied every one of her rooms, that is.

"Okay." Sabra turned to EV, "It's over. I'm sorry for tossing snow on you. Come in and I'll get you cleaned up." Lottie would have made the offer if she hadn't been thinking of other things. Sure enough, though, Lottie watched EV and Chloe follow Sabra inside where, no doubt, they would probably spend half an hour cackling with the witch about what a horrible person Lottie was and making sure Sabra's guests felt the same.

There was nothing left for her to do but go inside and try to dispel bad impressions based on what had just happened. Just her luck, the earth wasn't likely to open up and swallow her whole so she could avoid the next few minutes.

As it always did, walking into her business gave her a feeling of contentment. The decor in the main reception area managed to elevate the rustic method of building to something a bit more in keeping with Lottie's tastes. White shading to oatmeal graced the wall in the form of textile artwork; a woven piece gifted by the artist herself, Anna Zemaya—better known as EV Torrence's mother—not that Lottie would hold that against her. Anna was a class act. Those colors she'd matched in the sofa and decorative pillows. A small spotlight flicked its glow across an abstract diptych made of glass and metal in shades mimicking the flame from the energy-efficient fireplace insert below. Scarlet deepening through red to amber danced from left to right. Every time her gaze fell upon the piece, Lottie felt more alive.

Now, seated in front of that fireplace, several guests looked up as she entered the room. Every drop of saliva turned to dust and glued her mouth closed. Words fled her mind like rats leaving a sinking ship. In the end, she could only stand and wait for what came next.

"I like the white decor," said the pretty, blond half of a couple in their mid-thirties. "It's restful to the eye." Her name, Lottie remembered, was Paula. "We were thinking of coming back for your spring celebration next month. Can we make a reservation for that now?"

With gratitude, Lottie made a note of it in her book. "All set."

Chapter 10

"Nate, we got something!" Dalton burst through the office door to find his partner poring over Stacey's case files, photos of the crime scene spread out in front of him. His head rested in his hands, and when he looked up it was with bloodshot eyes indicating a lack of restful sleep.

"Finally!" Nate quickly shuffled some papers and stuffed the lot back into a crisp manila folder. "Show me."

"Did you know Stacey was an up-and-coming prosecuting attorney in Boston before she moved back to Gilmore about eighteen months ago? Boston University Law School; top of her class. Her mother is a homemaker, and her father is going on forty years at the post office. She had to have paid her own way, unless there's some unknown, wealthy benefactor. Who would go through all that, just to leave it all behind to return to small-town living?" Dalton couldn't understand how he could be suffering from verbal incontinence with his foot jammed firmly in his mouth, but Nate's raised eyebrow quickly turned into a sheepish grin.

"It happens, man, I'm living proof. But you're right; it's unusual. Something must have happened…" Nate trailed off, his detective side kicking in and making the connection. "And that's why her laptop and briefcase were stolen; it's work-related, just like we thought. We need more information."

"The DA's office sent over a list of Stacey's cases, but that's all they'll release without more to go on. Let's see…she was third chair on a big tax evasion case shortly before resigning. Rumored mob ties—oh, wouldn't Zellner have a field day with that one—but it seems pretty open and shut. Prior to that—this sounds a bit more promising—a domestic violence case involving strangulation." Nate's eyebrows rose at the word 'strangulation' but he remained silent, so Dalton continued. "And the one before that involved contract disputes for a local manufacturer's union."

"You're right, the second one sounds promising, but we don't want to leave any stone unturned."

"It's going to be a long night, isn't it?"

"Yep, I'll call Chloe and let her know we'll be burning the midnight oil. And I'll order us some food. Might as well settle in. If these don't net us a solid lead we'll keep digging, but for now I'm going to reach out to my buddy from the academy, Tim McReady. He's a detective in South Boston. Maybe he'll have a bit more insight for us."

"Don't even think about ordering another pizza; you must have marinara sauce running through your veins at this point. I'll bring you both dinner in about an hour." Chloe assured Nate. While she would have offered to bring him dinner whether she thought there was any information to be gained or not, but she wasn't so benevolent that the idea had escaped her attention.

Guys caught a break—working late. Going to bring them dinner, and if I happen to gain some info...so be it! Chloe shot a text to EV. Moments later, the ping of her cell phone indicated a response.

Stuck at the co-op. Will send pics of Lottie's outfit—you'll die. Good luck! Call me later. Another ping, and Chloe was left wondering why a woman of considerable girth would ever willingly put her dimpled behind on display so prominently.

Leggings are not pants! Chloe replied, shaking her head to clear the offending image.

After puttering around in the kitchen for a quarter of an hour, Chloe pulled a pair of bright purple sheepskin-lined boots over thick fleece leggings—ignoring her earlier statement about their validity as pants—and donned a fuzzy leopard print hat topped with cat ears. A puffy cream-colored jacket completed the look. Cheeks flushed pink, her blue eyes glowing, she sneaked a quick look in the mirror and determined that she did, in fact, pull off the somewhat eccentric outfit. Besides, it wasn't as if Ponderosa Pines was known for haute couture. And, Lottie's butt was way bigger.

She tripped out the door, carting a large picnic basket in one hand and a small cooler in the other, and deposited both into the minuscule back seat of her battered Mini Cooper. It was too cold to walk, and the recent snowfall had yet to become packed down and navigable through her usual wooded trail.

Nate and Dalton's hunched-over silhouettes were visible as she parked outside their office. Her heart skipped a beat as she watched Nate catch sight of her approach and offer a devastatingly handsome grin. All he had to do was lean back in his chair to open the door and relieve her of her burden. She still couldn't quite believe she had gotten so lucky.

"Pastrami and Swiss on dark rye; red potato salad; and some monster cookie rice crispy treats. There are two different kinds of crushed cookies in those, and they're topped with mini M&Ms. Should keep you wired for a while. Oh, and I brought you guys some iced coffee and a couple of sodas—they're in the cooler."

Dalton unwrapped a thick sandwich and inhaled the scent of caramelized onions, spicy mustard, and tangy pickles with a faraway expression on his face. "How did you manage to put this all together at the last minute?" he asked Chloe incredulously through a mouthful of pastrami.

"Oh, most of that was leftovers; I just heated up the onions and made the sandwiches. Potato salad is always better the day after, anyway." She brushed off the compliment, but was secretly pleased. "Though, if you're grateful, I'd be willing to take payment in the form of information. What are you hunkering down to investigate?"

Nate wrapped his arms around Chloe's shoulders and pulled her in for a kiss that ended far too quickly for her liking. "Nice try, Love. I'd give you just about anything in exchange for food, but we've got a bet running, remember? You're just going to have to wait."

He didn't fail to notice her keen eyes roaming the room for clues, or miss the flicker of smugness she tried to cover after they lit upon his computer screen (currently open to the 'Steinke, Burns, and Pruitt' website). Chloe obviously thought she had gleaned a little bit of information; and he was sure she realized they were looking into Stacey's work life. What she would do with that information, though, he couldn't be 100% sure of.

After Chloe's tail lights had receded back in the direction from which she had come, Nate turned to Dalton. "Let them snoop around Gilmore; at least that'll keep them out of trouble. No reason to let on that this case might go back a lot further than that. No dice on my friend Tim; he wasn't in his office. I left a message, but in the meantime, we've got plenty here to sift through."

Juggling a clipboard, tape measure, and a purse big enough to hold camping supplies for a small army, Veronica dropped the key to the consignment shop into the snow at her feet. Why anyone bothered to lock it was beyond her to begin with. What was there to steal? The only thing left behind was a bunch of dusty old chairs. This space had served a number of functions over the years—first as a one-room schoolhouse to most recently as an annex to the co-op while the complex that housed it was under expansion. It was an honor to become the next tenant; one that Veronica felt deeply.

After a minute of groping, Veronica pulled the key out of the snow and unlocked the door, knowing Mindy would be late, as usual. It never failed to amuse Veronica how Mindy was considered the grounded one between the two of them while she, herself, was labeled as dingy more often than not. Yet, Mindy would be late to her own funeral, while Veronica never missed an appointment.

According to her watch, she had at least a half hour before Mindy Time caught up with the rest of the world; just enough to scoot over to The Mudbucket for a tall mocha. In the few moments it had taken to divest herself of all but the voluminous purse, the streets had started to fill up with students on their way to the first tour of the day. Veronica was on the schedule for working three of the tours this year, and she looked forward to it—less so than the coffee-slinging shifts Talia had tagged her for. Remembering orders correctly just wasn't her thing.

The sound of a snowmobile coming closer pulled Veronica out of her reverie just before she saw Harley Moffett come rocketing down through the middle of town on his Ski-do. No helmet, ears red with cold, eyes redder with drink—and at this time of day, too—he paid no attention whatsoever to the pedestrians clogging the narrow road as he whooped and hollered on his way through. They scattered like tenpins in a bowling alley ahead of him. Chet Morgan ended up on the bottom of a small pile of bodes right in front of her. With no consideration, he shoved his way out from under a petite brunette, tossed off a few words that made her cheeks turn pink, then shot to his feet. Veronica tried to help brush the snow off his coat, but he glared at her with fury and stalked off in the direction he'd been going. What lovely manners.

"Is anyone hurt?" She called out before rushing to check for casualties.

By some miracle, other than a couple of scratches and a bruise or two, the general populace remained unscathed. Coffee forgotten, Veronica was still reassuring college students when Mindy arrived.

"Let me guess. Harley Moffett." This was not the

first time Harley had mounted such an offense. He was well known in town for playing chicken with tourists.

"Got it in one."

"Anyone hurt? Did you call Nate?"

"Not badly. Bumps mostly. And yes, Detective Hottie came and hauled old Harley off the sled. I'm sure he's sleeping it off somewhere right now. You're late, by the way."

Mindy checked her watch. "No, I'm not."

"Whatever, let's go take a look at what we have to work with before I have to show up for tour duty." Veronica linked her arm through Mindy's. At the spot where Chet Morgan had landed on his excellent ass, Veronica's foot connected with something hidden under a layer of snow loosened by the track of Harley's sled.

"What's this?" She reached down to fish a cell phone out of the wet and cold. "Someone lost their phone." She keyed up the power button, but the screen only flashed once and then went out. "Must have gotten wet." Mindy followed Veronica through the door of their new venture and watched in awed wonder as the enormous purse yielded a zipper bag full of rice.

"What else you got in there?" Mindy angled to try and get a peek. No matter what happened, Veronica could pull something out of there to help. "Come on, Mary Poppins, show me what's in the bag," she teased.

"Hey, you drop your phone in a public toilet enough times, you do what you gotta."

"How many times is enough?" Veronica scowled at her grinning friend.

"Once, really. But I've done it three times now. Hence the bag of rice."

"Hence." A sage nod was all Mindy dared. Hapless though she might seem, Veronica had a knack for making insightful comments, because she always managed to see right through the bull to the truth underneath—and she got testy when she thought others were making fun of her.

Into the bag went the phone and the whole thing disappeared into the depths of Veronica's purse where out of sight, it went right out of her mind. "What do you think about putting a small changing room in this corner?"

Chapter 11

Chloe rested her head in one hand and used the other to rub the water out of her eyes. Two hours scouring Stacey's Facebook, Instagram, and Twitter accounts had yielded nothing but a niggling headache, and the impression that Stacey Hawthorne's personal life included nothing remotely sinister or macabre. Unless it was a fondness for squirrel images. There must have been a hundred of them.

I've got to be missing something.

Failure wasn't something Chloe just accepted; she pushed through and found a way—always. It didn't occur to her that this should be any different. Stacey had been heading for the Pines, possibly intending to stay in town for a couple of days. None of her business here seemed of dire enough importance to force her out in the blizzard of the decade. One thing that kept coming back to Chloe was the notion that strangulation was a crime most often committed for reasons of a personal nature. In that context, it was possible her briefcase and phone had been taken in an attempt to throw suspicion onto Stacey's work life.

Chloe knew Nate and Dalton were researching the professional aspect; it only made sense for her and EV to focus on the personal. With that in mind, Chloe chose to respond exactly as she would if she were researching a tip for her column, 'Babble & Spin'. Usually, social media held some clue (provided she looked hard enough), but Stacey clearly wasn't the type to post every minute detail of her life for all to see.

In the back of Chloe's mind, she could hear her editor, Wesley, encouraging her to dig deeper—get out from in front of the computer and observe real life firsthand. Which would be a lot easier if Stacey wasn't lying unconscious at County General.

Speaking of Wesley, Chloe knew he was expecting her next column ASAP. It was closer to deadline than she had ever submitted in the past, and she was surprised he wasn't breathing down her neck already.

The *Pine Cone*, Ponderosa Pines' weekly newsletter, was a passion project of Wesley's; one he took very seriously. His uncle Vic, one of the earliest town residents, started the *Cone* when the Pines was still a commune. In fact, he was the original Miss Busybody —a title Chloe now held as the anonymous 'Babble & Spin' author—though she doubted anyone had been fooled during those early years. Since then, several authors had come and gone, and Vic eventually decided to live out his twilight years in a Florida condo. One with a ratio of 2 women for every man. With those odds, he was sure to score.

Wesley, having spent most of his childhood summers in the Pines, couldn't bear the thought of shutting down the newsletter, or allowing Vic to sell his house; instead, he came back to the town he remembered with great fondness and feelings of home to continue his uncle's work. Chloe could relate; and in fact, the kindred nature of their feelings toward the tiny town was what kept Chloe churning out column after column.

Deciding a break was in order, she added another paragraph to the nearly finished piece and headed back into the cold to drop the paper copy off to him in person. When she arrived, the re-purposed storage pod office Wesley worked out of was dark. With

WHaC going on, the chances of running into someone increased tenfold, so Chloe dropped the column into his mailbox and hurried back to her side of town. At least it was done, and now maybe he wouldn't realize how close she had cut it.

Chloe parked in her driveway and hurried around the back of the house, trudging across the deep snow and through a break in the fence between her backyard and EV's.

"Perfect timing, I just got in." EV said with a smile as Chloe tumbled through her back door. "Want some tea?" she asked while filling the ancient, dented teapot Chloe knew was one of EV's prized possessions.

"Always." She responded, settling into a padded dining chair and filling EV in on the events of her day.

"Dalton and Nate have much easier access to Stacey's work files; there's no way we can compete. But while they're focusing on that, I thought it would be a good idea to look into her personal life." Chloe explained. "But I checked her profiles and came up with bupkis."

"Well, what do you know, there are still people who value privacy in this world. Has there been any word on her condition? Maybe we should take a trip to County, see for ourselves how she's doing. Maybe there's a visitor log we can peek at." EV suggested.

"Sounds like a plan. Tomorrow afternoon?"

"Perfect. It's a date. Now, did you hear about the kerfluffle at New Sage this morning?"

"No, I've been in research mode all morning. What happened?" A second teaspoon of sugar went into Chloe's tea along with a dollop of thick cream.

"It was Lottie and Sabra again. Go figure. The way I heard it, they grabbed for the same bag of flour, and by the time it was all over Rainn had a mess on her hands." EV tossed over her shoulder while she grabbed a container of homemade cookies from the cupboard.

"What is it with those two? There has to be more to it than just a business rivalry. Did they fight over a boy in school or something?" Chloe selected a cookie from the plate.

"They were both a few years behind me in school, so I'm not sure if there was more to it, but I think this all stems back to a fight over who won first place in their age division of the town talent show when they were in sixth or seventh grade."

Mouth dropping open, Chloe said, "You're kidding, right?"

"No, sadly not. Lottie twirled a mean baton, Sabra yodeled, and when it came time to vote by the sound of applause, the judges deemed it too close to count so they called it a tie."

The mental image sent Chloe into a bout of laughter. Unfortunately, she had just taken a bite of cookie and nearly choked. EV slapped her on the back. When she could breathe again, Chloe wished, "Too bad that was before the days of cell phone video cams."

A wicked grin lighting her face, EV said, "Yeah, but you're forgetting one thing, Super 8."

"No way. Are you telling me you have a copy?"

In answer, EV waggled her eyebrows. "With sound and all."

"I have to see that footage. You have a projector, I've seen it somewhere. Come on, don't hold out on me. What were they wearing? Tell me Sabra had on Lederhosen. And Lottie? I'm picturing something sparkly and little white boots. Oh, and her hair all teased up and poofy. I seriously have to see this film. Is there time before we're due for tour duty?"

"That depends. Do you want the modern version or do you need the full ambiance? I had all the old reels converted to VHS back in the day, and then when DVD came along...you know how I like to keep current."

"Both. DVD now, so you can fast forward to the salient parts, but I totally have to see it in the original format. We're going to forgo game night for a home movie marathon this week. Is that the only one you have? Is my mom on it? I'd love to see her back then."

Realizing she should have thought of this before, EV motioned for Chloe to follow, then led her to a set of built-in cabinets that extended from floor to ceiling in the far corner of the living room. She threw open the right hand door to expose shelves of old media.

"I've got a whole video library here. It'll take more than one Friday night showing to cover them all."

Chapter 12

"It's dangerous, Carrie." Dalton's blood pressure raised enough to redden his face in reaction to his daughter's announcement. She flitted from one thing to another these days, each more dangerous than the last.

EV made a move to leave the room in order to allow Dalton and his daughter more privacy, but he pulled her back down to sit beside him. Though the signs were subtle, EV could tell Carrie wasn't entirely on board with her father's new relationship. Studied politeness couldn't hide the set of her mouth, or the way Carrie's eyes never quite met EV's. Dalton appeared unaware of the undercurrents. Odd, EV thought, since he tended to be more alert to nuance in his dealings with people.

"It's perfectly safe, Dad. Hundreds of people volunteer through the organization every year. I thought you'd be a little more open to new experiences now that you've decided to restart your own life by moving in a totally different direction. It takes a sense of adventure to become a cop at your age." She left the part about finding a new woman unsaid, but EV heard it loud and clear.

"Becoming a deputy in Ponderosa Pines is nothing like spending twelve weeks saving wildlife in Costa Rica." His wry tone drew a snort from EV—which, in turn, drew the hint of an eye roll from Carrie. Some days those two things were not as far apart as he might think. Riding herd on the likes of Harley Moffett could qualify as herding wild animals.

"I thought you'd be proud of me. I've taken a temporary leave of absence from my job, and I'm not asking you to pay for anything."

"You know I'm proud of you. Of course, I am. But why can't you find a way to help animals without going to the ends of the earth where I can't protect you?"

"Costa Rica is hardly the ends of the earth."

"I'm going to take my evening walk and let the two of you hash this out." This time when Dalton tried to stop her, EV avoided his grasping hand. Father and daughter needed to talk. Alone. Still, she couldn't resist tossing out one last comment toward the younger woman. "I think it would be a fantastic experience for you."

"Like I care what she thinks." Carrie's muttered comment earned her a stern look from Dalton.

"She's been nothing but nice to you, so back off, Carrie." His tone softened, "I don't remember you giving your mother such a hard time when she decided to take up with Denise, and you hadn't even had a chance to meet her. You've known EV your whole life, and I always thought you liked her. Unless you've been listening to Summer Daniels and that poison tongue of hers."

The attitude slipped away with a sigh. "I'm just afraid she's going to hurt you. Her track record with relationships speaks for itself. Love 'em and leave 'em."

Dalton found himself stuck in the middle of a dilemma. Carrie deserved to know certain information about the woman he intended to marry as soon as he could talk her into agreeing, but him telling that information would violate EV's privacy. In the end, he settled for a cryptic comment.

"EV had her reasons for the way she lived her life before. If you ask her, I'm sure she'll explain." Letting the topic go, he returned to the one uppermost in his mind.

"Tell me more about Costa Rica. What exactly will you be doing there?"

"The first week we'll be taking orientation classes. I already speak Spanish so I'll have a leg up on that. When that's over, we're going to work with wild animals that have been hurt or displaced. The intention is to make them healthy and release them back into the wild. Brice says…" Carrie broke off before finishing the sentence.

"Brice?" That cleared up a lot. "I take it you're not going alone?"

"Dad, Brice is just a friend."

Dalton read between those lines well enough. All the signs were there—cheeks dusted with color; eyes shining; he even noted the elevated pulse at her throat. Nate's lessons in observation were rubbing off.

Carrie's excited recitation halted when a cold breeze swirled in behind a pink-cheeked EV. Kicking off snow-covered boots, she crossed to warm nearly numb fingers in front of the fire. The fond look she tossed Dalton's way, and his in return, did not go unnoticed by Carrie. Her heart softened slightly, even though she wasn't ready to admit she'd been wrong. Growing up in Ponderosa Pines, serving coffee at The Mudbucket during her teen years, and living above it to save money throughout college had given her plenty of chances to get to know EV. Everything she remembered about the woman pointed to her being a kind and helpful person. After Costa Rica, Carrie decided, she'd take time to have that talk her dad had suggested.

"I don't like it," Sitting at the desk pushed up against the back of the sofa upon which EV currently reclined, Dalton spun the laptop around so she could see the website cued up in his browser. "I don't want my daughter working with wild animals in a remote region of the country. It's not safe. What if she gets hurt? Or lost?" He returned the computer to its original position and continued looking through the site.

"She's twenty-five years old."

"Twenty-six," Dalton corrected absently, his focus still on the images scrolling across his screen. "Did you know she's going there with some guy named Brice?"

"Ah, so that's what's got your panties in a twist."

"Panties?" Taking mock offense, Dalton refused

to give up his main point. "She's chasing some guy into the wilderness. She says they're just friends."

"Maybe they are. And if they aren't, it's still a great experience for her. Didn't you ever want to have an adventure?"

"You mean other than taming you?"

"Very funny. That'll take a lifetime. Now, show me those panties," EV circled the sofa to roll Dalton's chair back from the desk and plop into his lap. He'd happily give up his lifetime to that pursuit.

Sometime after midnight, while she slogged through the to-do list her father had sent—EV was in charge, reluctantly, of running the website for her family's charitable foundation—her Skype app dinged. Chloe kept late hours almost as often as EV did.

What are you still doing up? —Chloe
Web stuff.

Was it completely crazy to chat over the Internet when only a few hundred steps separated the two homes? It was cold out and EV needed to vent, so she clicked the video chat button. When Chloe's face swam onto the screen, EV giggled to see the younger woman's hair tied up in a bandanna while what looked like an oatmeal face mask covered her face. She looked like a reverse raccoon.

"Wipe that look off your face, we can't all have skin like a baby's butt."

"I needed the comic relief. Carrie hates me and I have no idea why."

"She's probably just being protective of her dad."

EV gave her the rundown, let Chloe cheer her up, and went to bed feeling considerably lighter.

Chapter 13

"It feels wrong to show up without a gift, or flowers or something." EV whispered to Chloe as they rode the elevator up to Community General Hospital's third floor intensive care unit.

"What did you want to do, bake her a casserole? The poor woman is in a coma; and I doubt the first words out of her mouth will have anything to do with proper etiquette. Besides, it's Christian I'm worried about; Stacey is being monitored by a team of doctors and nurses, but nobody's looking after him, and I don't think he's been back home since the night of her attack."

"I know; Zellner of all people has been keeping an eye on his place. Seems he's gotten over Christian stealing the clothes off his scarecrow; I don't think he's ever forgiven a faux pas quite so quickly." EV shook her head; she'd tried to get on Zellner's good side for years, to no avail. It probably had something to do with the fact that EV had no patience for Abe's conspiracy theories, or his tendency toward impromptu, informative lectures. Christian, on the other hand, seemed to enjoy them, and with his enthusiasm had stroked Zellner's ego into submission.

Rounding the corner into Stacey's room, Chloe let out a low whistle. "I guess we needn't have worried about Christian." A tray of food sat next to a fold-out chair made into a bed, and though his face was drawn in concern, his clothes and hair were clean and recently washed.

"Hey Christian, how are you?" Chloe asked as she enveloped the man in a comforting hug.

"How's Stacey?" EV asked at the same time. She glanced over to the bed where Stacey was hooked up to several beeping machines with an IV of something clear running into the crook of her elbow, her blank face somehow peaceful in sleep

Christian shook his head sadly. "She still hasn't regained consciousness, but she's stable. And she's breathing on her own, which is a very good sign." He sunk onto a chair and reached out to stroke Stacey's fingers.

"Have you been here the whole time?" EV asked gently. "What about her family? Has she had a lot of visitors?"

"I haven't been home, no. But the nurses here have been bringing me things ever since they realized I wasn't going to leave. There's an undercover officer stationed in the hallway, but I still don't feel comfortable leaving, in case the guy who did this tries to finish the job." He stared down at the dainty hand resting inside his larger, stronger one. "I just wish I could have gotten there a few minutes faster. It seems I'm always a bit too late."

"You did as much as you could, and more than most people would have done. She's extremely lucky. Stay positive; that's what she needs right now."

Relaxing infinitesimally, Christian began to open up and gestured to the food and blankets piled around him. "Stacey's parents are the nicest people; they've given me permission to stay as long as I like, and even talked the nurses into lifting the visiting hours ban."

Chloe and EV exchanged a knowing glance. Christian's history included the unsuccessful rescue attempt of a child trapped in a burning building. Unnecessary guilt had taken a toll on his mental health, and it seemed he was pinning a lot of hope for redemption on Stacey's recovery. Whether that was healthy for him or not, it was his truth.

"Christian, we're trying our best to find out who did this—and of course, the police are working tirelessly as well. Have you seen anyone suspicious poking around Stacey's room?"

"Well, I did see a man here the other day, but I'm not even sure if he was coming to see Stacey. He walked back and forth in the hallway a couple of times and then left. I assumed he was in the wrong place, but the more I think about it, it seemed like he was trying too hard to not be noticed."

"What did he look like?"

"I didn't really get a good look at him. He kept his face turned slightly away at all times. And yet, something about him seemed vaguely familiar. Tall, brown hair with a tinge of red to it, kind of a square jaw, wire-rimmed glasses, and he was wearing jeans under a button-down shirt. I feel like I've seen him before, and I think I'd recognize him if I saw him again."

"Thank you, Christian. Is there anything you need—can we bring you something?"

Christian shook his head sadly. "No, there's nothing I need, but now that you mention it…"

"Anything…" EV encouraged.

"Stacey's cat, Triscuit, got loose when her mother and father went over to feed him. They're trying to get him to come back inside, but he's being stubborn. Would you be willing to go give them a hand so they can get back here? It's not far from here and I know they'd appreciate the help."

Chloe couldn't believe their good luck; a perfect excuse to poke around Stacey's apartment had just fallen into their laps. "Of course, Christian. What's her address."

"82 Water Street. Apartment 3B. I'll let Mr. and Mrs. Hawthorne know to expect you." And with that he went back to staring into Stacey's face while EV and Chloe exited quietly.

"Am I imagining things, or does that seem a bit extreme, even for Christian?" Chloe asked EV when they had returned to the parking garage and clambered into EV's pickup truck.

Chloe's eyes widened as she nodded in agreement. "Yes, it does. I hope Stacey wasn't dating anyone—though, if she was, you think he'd have stopped by the hospital—because Christian is seriously crushing hard, and he hasn't even really met her. I just hope she's as lovely as everyone seems to think. I'd hate for him to get his heart broken."

"We can worry about that later. Right now, we have other things to deal with. Like purchasing a lottery ticket, because apparently we have pleased the gods in some way today. Though I have to say, this is the strangest situation I think I've been in for at least a decade."

"I second that."

Pete and Mary Hawthorne turned out to be exactly how Christian described them: the nicest people in the world. Even racked with worry over their only daughter, the two were gracious and appreciative as Chloe coaxed a large yellow tiger cat from a crawlspace beneath the covered porch along the apartment building's south face. It had taken EV less than ten minutes to find him cowering there.

Chloe buried her hands in soft, toffee-colored belly fur and stroked the purring bear-cat's chin while he batted gently at her arm with his fuzzy mitten paws. *Oh, I would take you home, you big, fat baby.*

"We can't thank you enough. Stacey would be so upset if anything happened to this little guy." Mary gushed once they were standing in Stacey's kitchen watching Triscuit rub his plump belly against a half empty food dish. He looked up at the four of them expectantly.

"It's no problem, really. Christian is a good friend of ours, and although I don't know Stacey well, everyone has had nothing but good things to say about her. Chloe's fiancé is actually the lead detective on Stacey's case. He's been working day and night to try and figure out what happened." EV offered with a reassuring smile.

Chloe allowed her to take the reins, exploiting the opportunity to look around Stacey's apartment. The woman had obviously traveled extensively; Chloe could spot a kindred soul. Bright, multi-colored curtains livened up plain white walls, which were barely visible anyway between frames of eclectic art. A bohemian vibe echoed throughout the space, totally at odds with Chloe's preconceived notion of Stacey The Lawyer.

"I still can't believe someone would do this to our little girl. That young man, Christian—he's our miracle, the way he helped our Stacey like that. He doesn't even know her, and he won't leave her side." Pete's voice cracked and he squeezed his wife's tiny hand as if the wind might carry him away without her there to anchor him. Chloe cocked an ear to listen to the conversation and judge how much time she would have to snoop.

EV asked a couple more questions, giving Chloe a few more precious moments. She glanced around the living and dining rooms, and peeked her head into Stacey's bedroom. By the time she made her way back to the kitchen, Triscuit's food dish had been filled and the conversation was coming to a close.

"...asked if we could stop by and pick up the cat because she was going out of town for a few days. Something to do with an old case. He slipped past us the minute we opened the door, but he's here now."

"Mrs. Hawthorne, do you know if Stacey was dating anyone?" Chloe blurted out, her face reddening as she realized how invasive the question must seem. She needn't have worried; the woman was so distraught she barely noticed.

"No, not for a while. There was a man about eight months back, but it didn't work out. She didn't seem too upset about it; I got the feeling it was a mutual breakup."

"You don't know his name by any chance, do you?" Chloe prodded gently.

"Hmm, it started with a W. Walter, Wyatt...no, Wesley. I don't know his last name."

Chloe's eyes widened in surprise; that was the last name she expected to hear. Christian's description coupled with Wesley's unprecedented absence the day before was too much of a coincidence. It all worked together to fuel Chloe's suspicion that her editor knew more about Stacey than he was letting on.

Once back outside, Chloe and EV bid goodbye to the hospital-bound Hawthornes before trudging around the building toward where they had parked on the far side of the lot. As they rounded the corner, and before Chloe and EV could exchange more than an alarmed look, a frail-looking old woman flagged them down.

"Hello dears, did you find that nice girl's cat?"

EV's eyes brightened; this was exactly what they needed: a nosy neighbor who would probably be more than willing to part with some information.

"Why, yes, we did find him. What a cute little guy; though, *little* is probably a stretch. I've never seen a cat that big before." EV let loose an exaggerated shiver.

"Are you ladies cold? Would you like a cup of tea?

The kettle is near to boiling, and I just pulled a batch of blueberry muffins out of the oven."

Jackpot.

"That would be lovely. I'm EV Torrence, by the way. And this is Chloe LaRue."

"Nice to meet you. My name is Louise. Come on in."

She led them to a first floor unit positioned beneath and to the right of Stacey's. The layout was a mirror image of the injured woman's apartment, everything exactly the same, but flipped to the other side. The stark white walls told Chloe that tenants weren't allowed to paint, which seemed a shame considering the rooms were actually quite nice, with none of the cheap, bargain bin fixtures typically found in apartment buildings.

Louise ushered them into the living room and gestured for them to take a seat on a gaudy, flowered couch. "I love cats, but my budgies don't." She pointed to large cage in the corner where two parakeets hopped enthusiastically over a set of ladders crisscrossing the enclosure.

"So, it's a shame about your neighbor, Stacey." Chloe hedged.

"Yes, I can't imagine why someone would want to hurt that poor girl. Did you know her well?"

"I'd met her once or twice before she was attacked on our town line, and Chloe's fiancé is the lead detective on her case. We stumbled into helping find the cat, but to be honest, we're mostly just being nosy." EV explained.

Louise didn't comment on that, but it was clear she was a fellow busybody, more than willing to discuss other people's business. "Stacey moved in almost a year and a half ago. She doesn't have many people in and out, and she's friendly but not *too* friendly, if you know what I mean." Louise supplied without any further prompting.

EV nodded sagely. "Yes, I do. So, nobody has been coming and going lately?" She prodded, hoping Louise understood her meaning.

"There was a man, a few months ago, who came by a few times. He seemed nice, but I could tell he wasn't the right man for her. They didn't have that sizzle, if you know what I mean."

Chloe grinned a response.

"Do you know his name? Or can you describe him?" Chloe asked, hoping there was another man Stacey's parents were unaware of. The last thing she wanted to do was investigate a friend and respected colleague.

"I never heard his name. And he was just a regular-looking man. Always dressed in slacks and loafers; tall, with dark hair and bushy eyebrows. Strong jaw. Nothing out of the ordinary." Then Louise dropped a bomb. "He was here the other night. I have an excellent view of the parking area from out of my bedroom window, and with all those street lights it's lit up like daylight out there. I had to buy those curtains that block out light, or I'd never get any sleep."

"And this was a few nights ago? Do you remember when exactly?"

"The night after her accident. I was getting ready for bed and went to the window to close the curtains. He came up the walk, and being curious, I kept the curtains open and watched. A few minutes later he came back down and left. You don't think he could have had anything to do with the attack, do you? He seemed like a nice, polite man." She shook her head sadly. "What a shame."

"Seriously, Wesley?" Chloe moaned when they had declined a third cup of tea and any more discussion of Louise's budgies, and were heading back to

Ponderosa Pines. "That's the second person to have seen someone fitting his description."

"You're right; Wesley doesn't fit the disgruntled ex-boyfriend profile. But we can't ignore the fact that someone has been skulking around. Do you think he'd talk to you? You do have a personal relationship."

"It's the most solid lead we have right now; I don't have a choice other than to try. If he's hiding anything, I'll know."

Chapter 14

"Harper here." Nate absentmindedly answered his cell phone on the second ring, his attention trained on the open case file spread across his desk.

"Hello, Nathaniel, it's Javier." Chloe's new stepfather greeted him warmly.

"Nice to hear from you, Javi. How goes married life?"

"It's wonderful, wonderful. We are busy decorating the beach house; the weather is beautiful this time of year. Lila does laps in the pool every morning. She'd really love it if you and Chloe would come visit." Javier cajoled. He was thrilled that all was well, and touched by the way Chloe's newly-extended family had embraced him.

"Well, we're right in the middle of blizzard season, so maybe we *should* take a trip to see you two. The cold, sunless days are taking their toll. Every time it snows, my shoulder injury starts to act up. And it snows every day! But you didn't call to hear me complain about the weather. What's going on?"

"You got me, I do have an ulterior motive. My brother Tomas' condition has improved greatly since you helped clear his name and put Remy Vincent away. He's going to be taking over Garritek sooner than expected, and he has his eye on the American market. I promised Lila I was retiring, and though she realizes I'll need to assist Tomas for a bit longer, he's going to be looking for a right-hand man in the States. Of course we both thought of you, especially since Lila mentioned that your post in Ponderosa Pines isn't permanent...Is it something you would even consider, or do you already have a line on another job?"

Have I been sending silent distress signals so strong they reached the Mediterranean? Nate wondered. Aside from Stacey's case, and of course Chloe, the major recurring thought on Nate's mind was what to do when Dalton permanently took over as the Pines' only resident police officer. Javi's offer couldn't have come at a more opportune time, but a multi-million-dollar startup was definitely a full-time-plus proposition that would undoubtedly require a lot of travel and little time at home. He wondered fleetingly whether Chloe had clued Lila in on his current state of ennui.

Nate sighed. "It's an intriguing prospect. I'd love to hear more about it."

Still, it couldn't hurt to get more information. Nate listened to Javier ramble happily, drinking in the possibility his future father-in-law offered. After he finally bid goodbye, Nate's head was in such a tailspin that he didn't answer the office phone until it had rung at least five times.

"Harper here." He repeated for what felt like the millionth time that day.

"It's Tim McReady returning your call." His voice was cold and unfamiliar, and Nate had to wonder if he even realized they had been previously acquainted.

"Do you remember me? We went to the police academy together..." Nate ventured.

"Of course, I never forget a name. You wanted to know about a couple of old cases? Didn't you get the files our department sent over?" He continued, his tone still brusque and unfriendly.

Nate blanched, but shook it off; who knows, the guy could have a stack of cases on his desk. "Yes, and

I noticed you were involved with at least two of those cases; is there anything that stands out as odd to you about any of the three? And did you happen to meet a Stacey Hawthorne? She was an attorney with the DA."

"Stacey, Stacey, no, that name doesn't sound familiar." Tim muttered absentmindedly, and Nate could make out the sound of papers shuffling in the background.

"Well, Ms. Hawthorne was attacked and strangled nearly to death a few nights ago, and we have reason to believe the motive might have been related to her work in Boston. Can you think of any reason why someone involved in those cases might want to hurt her?"

"Not off the top of my head, but I'd probably begin with the domestic violence; a woman was strangled in that case, if I remember correctly. Seems the most obvious place to start."

Nate could hear the silent 'duh' he was sure Tim had added, but decided to take the high road. "Thanks, Tim. Let me know if anything else comes to mind."

Chloe hummed to herself as she bustled about the kitchen, sidestepping her two playful Siamese cats, Sugar and Spice as they batted yet another pipe cleaner across the floor. Veronica's children had raided her craft cabinet weeks ago, and every time she thought she had retrieved the last of the fuzzy, flexible sticks another one turned up, usually in the cats' water dish.

"Shoo, you two." She chastised lightly, pulling a catnip-infused mouse from a bag under the sink and chucking it into the living room. "Go play in there for a bit."

For the last hour, Chloe had been mixing dough and pressing it through the pasta attachment of her standing mixer to create strand after strand of golden tagliatelle. Wild mushrooms simmered in an aromatic garlic and thyme butter sauce, and a bottle of pinot noir rested in a decanter for Nate's arrival.

The sound of scampering kittens let her know Nate was home; their current catnip buzz increased the usual level of rambunctiousness, and when he stepped into the kitchen it was with a cat on each shoulder.

"I think these little guys are part parrot. Why do they only do this to me?" Nate wondered as he carefully detached himself and sent Sugar and Spice back out of the kitchen with a quick rub behind each tiny ear.

"I don't know, they just love you." Chloe laughed. "How was your day?"

"Considerably better now that I'm here with you." Nate wrapped his arms around Chloe's waist and lifted her into a head-spinning kiss. She couldn't believe they'd spent so much time as friends; the chemistry between them was palpable, and it was hard to fathom how they had ignored it for so long.

"What smells so good?" Nate's question jostled Chloe from her reverie.

"Homemade tagliatelle with mushrooms, garlic, and thyme; crusty artisan bread with a crushed pepper olive oil dipping sauce; and chocolate hazelnut cannoli for dessert. No big deal."

"Is this a bad news thing or a good news thing?" Nate teased. "Whenever you go to town in the kitchen, there's something on your mind. Not that I'm complaining; it sounds amazing and I'm starved. Is that wine?"

Chloe nodded and poured him a glass, standing on her tiptoes to peck him on the lips as she handed it over. "No news at all. I just needed a project and I wanted to use my new pasta maker. And I know we've been a little tense with everything that's happened—hence, the wine."

"Good call, I can't wait. I'll go get cleaned up for dinner."

By the time he returned, the table was set and dinner was served.

"This is amazing." Nate moaned after his first bite of earthy, butter-laden mushrooms and tender strands of pasta. They ate in silence for a while, allowing good food and good wine to soothe away the day's tension. "I got a call from Javi today."

"Oh, that's unusual. What did he have to say? Are he and my mom doing well?" Chloe's response put to rest Nate's niggling fear that she had anything to do with Javier's call.

"Yes, of course. Lila's redecorating the beach house and having a fabulous time. He did extend an offer for us to visit, which would be appealing if we hadn't just spent a month out of the country. But what he really wanted was to offer me a job working at Garritek with Tomas."

"Really? And what would that entail?" She knew before Nate could respond that it would mean a lot of travel, and that wasn't something she was excited about. Before coming back to Ponderosa Pines, Chloe spent years traveling around the globe with Lila; she had experienced that life already, and was happy to settle down and have a real home. She thought that was what Nate wanted as well, but maybe she was wrong. The idea was unsettling, but even so, she wouldn't dream of discouraging Nate from something that would make him happy.

"Garritek is already global, but they still operate solely out of the main office. Tomas wants to create a second division with a home base here in the states. If I want the job, they'll operate out of Gilmore, but I know that's more to suit my needs than their own. They'd do a lot better to settle on L.A. or New York City. One of the larger hubs. I can't see potential clients flying into Portland and then driving over an hour besides."

"No kidding. Factor in the weather and it seems a little foolhardy."

"Part of me is flattered at the offer; and even though it's a career trajectory I wasn't planning, it would be a step up in a lot of ways. But I don't get that tingly feeling about it—that spark of intuition that lets you know when something is right—it just isn't there."

Chloe chose her words carefully. "If it's what you

want, you should go for it. But if you're having reservations, maybe you need to take some time and really think about what would make you happy. Don't rush into anything."

"I know I need to figure out what my goals are; it's just that career-wise, everything is in question for me right now and that's terrifying." He leaned back in his chair, popped the last piece of moist bread into his mouth, and washed it down with a swig of wine. "For as long as I can remember, my path has been pretty straightforward. I've known I wanted to be a detective since...I can't remember when. And yet, I've never felt fulfilled; even when I was promoted, it felt hollow somehow. Not like I didn't deserve it, but more like it was too easy. I found myself gravitating toward the most complicated cases, searching for something deeper."

"And you didn't ever find what you were looking for?"

Nate rose to his feet and pulled Chloe into a tight embrace. "Not until the first time I kissed you. I've never felt more like I'm where I'm supposed to be, and as wonderful as that is, it makes the confusion about my career all the more vivid. Complicated as you are, loving you doesn't actually qualify as career status."

"Are you saying I'm a lot of work?" She leaned back to see his smirk and wrinkled up her nose. "I support whatever decision you make. I'm not super thrilled about the idea of you being gone all the time, but we can handle it if that's what you need to do."

Chloe deposited another firm kiss on his lips and gave his shoulder a squeeze before beginning to clear the table. Nate balanced three serving dishes and their dinner plates on one hand while Chloe wiped the table and stowed the leftovers in the refrigerator. They moved together seamlessly, as if they had been living together for years instead of a few short weeks. The thought calmed Chloe's nervous mind, and by the time they retired to the living room for some guilty pleasure reality television, she was once again confident that she and Nate would weather whatever storm might be headed their way.

Chapter 15

"Hey, Wesley, long time no see." Chloe ventured into the tiny building where Wesley was seated behind a high-tech computer setup featuring three separate monitors. Clicking furiously, he glanced up at Chloe with a bewildered expression on his face; she tended to avoid this space, seeing as how she was supposed to remain anonymous as the author of 'Babble & Spin'.

He pasted on a smile and turned to give Chloe his full attention. "What brings you here? Are you having trouble with the column?"

Chloe took a tentative seat across from Wesley and surveyed the man with new eyes. He looked normal, if a little worn out; red-rimmed eyes had her wondering if he was getting enough sleep, and his chestnut hair was mussed from pulling his fingers through it repeatedly.

"No, the column is fine. How are you doing?" She shifted uncomfortably as he muttered a 'good, good' and waved a hand to indicate she should continue. "I'm actually here on personal business."

"OK. What's going on? You're not quitting on me, are you?"

"No, of course not." She sighed and allowed the words to tumble out of her mouth. "I know it's really not my place to ask, but I was hoping you could tell me about your relationship with Stacey Hawthorne."

Wesley's bushy eyebrows shot up in surprise, and his chiseled jaw clenched momentarily. "Are you asking me as a friend, or as Nathaniel Harper's fiancée?"

"Nate doesn't know I'm here, and I have no intention of telling him anything about our conversation." *As long as you don't 5-alarm my sketch-o-meter.* She added silently.

Wesley seemed satisfied, and having no reason to doubt Chloe's word or ability to keep a secret, continued, "I haven't seen or talked to Stacey in about six months. We've known each other since we were 17; the summer between junior and senior year of high school." His expression took on a far-away quality as he recalled the feeling of youthful romance.

"She was incredible; smart and driven, already planning on studying pre-law and had her sights set on a high-profile job in the city after law school. We were kids, but I knew there was something special about her."

"What happened?" Chloe's voice broke through Wesley's reverie.

"We were young." He said, matter-of-factly. "And she moved to Boston right after graduation. I went off to Michigan State and didn't see her again until about...I don't know, ten months ago when she wandered past me in town; I thought I'd seen a ghost. We went out a few times, but it wasn't the same. She used to be carefree, confident. This time, she was timid, cautious, like the fire inside had burned out. I ended it before every happy memory I had of us was destroyed. It was a clean break, and we vowed to remain friends, although we haven't spoken since."

Chloe processed the deluge of information for a few moments, honing in on what she considered the most important bits. "What do you think caused such a big change in her?"

Wesley's gaze shifted away from her eyes, an action not unnoticed by Chloe, who waited patiently for his response. "Honestly, I think it had to do with a high-profile case she had been working on. I don't know the specifics; she would never tell me much, which I completely understood. Confidentiality, you know. But one night she got really upset, and when I pressed, she finally gave me the Reader's Digest version."

"Go on..." Chloe pressed

"Stacey became friends with someone involved in the case, someone who was in danger. It sounded like maybe this woman was a witness or something. Anyway, she kept saying she had to protect Alicia. I got the impression Stacey couldn't get a hold of Alicia, and was worried. That was all she would say, and she refused to talk about it again. We broke up shortly after that, and I haven't talked to her since."

If you're telling me the whole truth, I'll eat my own boot. She thought to herself. "You haven't dropped by her apartment recently? Or visited her in the hospital?" Chloe asked abruptly, eliciting a raised eyebrow from Wesley.

"No, like I said, I haven't seen her for about eight months and we didn't date long enough for me to even meet her parents, so I didn't think it was my place to go. Besides, I heard Christian is there and I didn't want to step on any toes." He sniffed, his change in demeanor giving off the air of a man who harbored some measure of jealousy about a woman he didn't even want for himself. That wasn't a good enough reason for wanting her dead, Chloe didn't think. It felt more like a bit of bruised pride than a dog marking territory.

Wesley turned his attention back to one of the computer screens. "Now, if you don't have any more questions, I've got to get back to finalizing this week's layout."

"Actually, just one more. Do you have any idea what other clients Stacey might have been visiting in Ponderosa Pines?" Chloe remained firmly seated, waiting expectantly for Wesley's answer.

"I think I heard Tank Daniels say he was working with her, and I gave her contact info to Allegra Worth after Ashton was sentenced. As for friends, I don't know of anyone in particular. Stacey didn't seem to have much of a social life these days. That might have changed over the last eight months, but I'd be the wrong person to ask."

Chloe finally rose and hedged toward the door. "Thanks, Wes. And I'm sorry to have intruded like this. I'd like to figure out who hurt her."

"Me too. Just because we aren't together anymore

doesn't mean I want anything bad to happen to her. Stacey's still a good person, and she didn't deserve this."

Chapter 16

Tank Daniels gestured toward the energy efficient stove he used to heat the one greenhouse he operated year-round for growing herbs and fresh salad ingredients. Fifteen students, four instructors, and both Lottie and Sabra, accompanied by a dozen or so of their current lodgers, milled around the narrow aisles between planting boxes.

"This is the combustion chamber. It's lined with fire block and a thick layer of mortar to increase thermal mass, which makes it an efficient source of heat. I added a simple copper coil along the first three feet of chimney to heat water, which is then piped through the soil to keep it warm. Lettuces require cooler soil, so they're at the end of the run, while plants that like warmer feet—peppers and tomatoes—are at the beginning. Running the tubing through the soil keeps the water insulated enough that when it returns to the tank, it's still warm." He popped open an observation door to show how it all worked. "I'm using a small pump to keep the water moving through the system. With the advent of LED grow lights, I can extend daylight by several hours without exceeding the power generated by a single wind turbine. Initial outlay was costly, but everything has paid for itself several times over."

"You paid for the lights? I thought this was a town where people only used what they could barter for or invent themselves." The bespectacled student made an observation, hitting on the biggest misconception outsiders had of Ponderosa Pines. Tank, always a champion for the town, made sure to divest him and anyone else of the false impression.

"No, son. We've got all the modern conveniences here." Tank's eyes twinkled, "Cell phones, Internet, cable TV. Our goal, as a town, is to find a way to live a modern life with as much energy efficiency as we can manage. Ponderosa Pines is the first town to generate more electricity than we can use. The rest is sold back to the power company, and the proceeds go toward expanding our own grid, as necessary."

While Tank continued to field questions and dispel crazy notions about the town, EV and Chloe handled their part of the presentation by manning the sampling table. A selection of vegetables harvested that morning glistened deliciously under the bright glare of LED lighting. When EV pulled out a pair of sunglasses, Chloe wrinkled her nose. The grow lights felt brighter than the sun and, had she thought ahead, the glasses would have been a welcome boon. "Got another pair of those?"

"Naturally."

Chloe accepted the rainbow-striped, over-sized glasses with equanimity. It was just like EV to be thoughtful enough to bring extras, and mean enough to make sure they were hideous.

"Cute. How do I look?"

"Like Elton John and Iris Apfel had a baby."

"You're just too funny for words." Pointing to a slice of beefsteak tomato that was easily the diameter of a softball, Chloe whispered, "I'm going to hit Tank up for a couple of these on my way out the door. They smell like summer." Her eyes turned wistful given the amount of snow still on the ground when spring was officially only two weeks away.

"You'll have to barter for them, according to that Harry Potter lookalike. What have you got to trade?

Some pumpkin pasties, or a mug of butterbeer, perhaps?"

"Sadly, nothing but a smile and some Bambi eyes," Chloe tipped down the glasses, grinned and gave EV a preview.

"Lucky for you, Tank is spoken for and won't be asking for personal favors." EV's mock leer garnered a withering stare from Nate who, along with Dalton, had been required by the town elders to maintain a low-key police presence at every tour. So far, the only rowdy participants had been Lottie and Sabra. The pair of them had attended every single presentation so far. And created a scene at better than half of them.

Lottie's attention remained riveted on Chet Morgan, who was among the attendees, while Sabra eyed the cucumbers on the sampling table with greed. Until Tank expanded his operation, something he'd already petitioned the town for help in doing, he didn't sell enough produce to fully satisfy Sabra's insatiable cucumber fetish. She'd come by to get a look at his grow light system with a view toward adding something similar to her own sunroom next winter.

Seemingly bored with the question and answer

period, the reporter made his way toward where Chloe and EV stood poised to offer a bite of something fresh. The way Chet Morgan's eyes roved over Chloe cranked Nate's already annoyed demeanor into a full-blown foul mood. It didn't get any better when he asked, "Don't I know you from somewhere?"

"No, I don't think so."

"Sure, I do. You're from Boston, right? It's been a couple years, but I'd recognize you anywhere, you've got one of those..." his gaze traveling down the length of her body made Nate's blood boil, "...faces."

His insistence on making a connection where none existed seemed odd. "I've lived in a lot of places, Boston isn't one of them." Chloe said dismissively. "You must have mistaken me for someone else."

Nate moved to intervene. "Is there a problem, Chloe?" He slung an arm around her as much for protection as to give the man a warning. Mine. Don't touch.

"I'm fine." Chloe laid a hand on Nate's arm. "It was just a mistake." Lowering her voice, she added, "No need to pee on me to mark your territory." Nate saw no humor in the flip remark.

Does she need every decent looking man in town chasing after her like a lovesick puppy? Lottie gave

Chloe the side eye—never mind that Chloe had done nothing to encourage Chet's unwanted attention. As usual, when anything threatened Lottie's equilibrium, she turned petulant.

"Come on, Talia. We're due over at The Mudbucket. Unlike some people," she turned pointed looks on EV, Chloe, and Sabra, "we're not too good to sully our hands serving coffee."

With a minimum of fuss, Tank ushered the tour participants outside—the students boarded waiting buses while he led the others on an unplanned excursion to observe the setup that powered his barn. A larger audience wouldn't do anything to diffuse the tense situation inside the greenhouse. When he had gone, only town members and the nosy reporter remained.

"Lottie," Allegra Worth joined the fray, "you're barking mad if you can't admit how hard everyone has worked to help Rhonda this past week." Broad *As* and dropped *Rs* betrayed Allegra's upbringing in eastern Massachusetts. Slightly strident, her tone attracted Chet Morgan's speculative eye, which only poured more fuel on Lottie's fire.

Opting to avoid being drawn into a battle of the

wits, EV merely treated Lottie to her best withering stare.

"Hush, now." Talia admonished her sister. "You're the one who told EV and Chloe their talents were more valuable elsewhere. And Sabra's done her part whenever I've asked. Just because I don't schedule the two of you together—and for very good reasons I might add—doesn't mean she's shirking."

A couple deep breaths could not quell Chloe's annoyance, and she felt a rant coming on until EV poked an elbow into her ribs and muttered, "Scale it down a notch, Ranty McGrumpypants. Talia's got this." Behind the dark lenses, Chloe's eyes narrowed to slits, but she subsided in favor of watching Lottie puff up over Talia's rebuke. Someone was sure to tip the scales soon—Chloe hadn't lost her temper in at least a few weeks—and EV figured there was someone out there besides Lottie who deserved her full attention.

"Talia knows she can count on me." Subtle emphasis indicating some kind of alliance between Sabra and Talia, combined with Chet's interest in yet another woman sent Lottie right over the edge.

"Anyone stupid enough to trust a backstabber like you deserves everything they have coming to them, but then again, my sister never was the brightest match in the pack." Stepping toe to toe with Sabra, Lottie thrust her considerable bosom forward in an aggressive stance. As one, Nate and Dalton moved to put a lid on the public display until EV threw out an arm to bar their way.

"Let it play out. Maybe they'll finally get it out of their system." An eyebrow waggle accompanied Chloe's offer of leftover veggies from the plate on the table, and Dalton could almost hear EV's wish for hot buttered popcorn and a comfy chair to watch the show. As it was, they stood around awkwardly, eating tomato slices topped with a sprinkling of freshly-snipped arugula and a drop of virgin olive oil.

"What exactly is your problem with me?" Sabra matched Lottie's posture. The pair of them reminded Chloe of the Zax in one of her favorite Dr. Seuss books. "I'd really like to know."

Scorn dripping from her tongue, Lottie sneered, "Don't hurt yourself trying to figure it out. It might require an original thought, and we all know you aren't scheduled for one of those until spring."

Taunts and insults flew like barbed arrows.

"Why don't you just go yodel." Even Lottie knew her comeback was lame.

"Oh," Sabra's mouth made the shape as the word left her lips. "Is that really what's been under your skin all this time? Because we tied at a talent show when we were kids?"

"Short memory. We were supposed to twirl batons together. I practiced that routine with you for a month, and at the last minute, without even saying a word, you dumped me and went on alone."

Sabra stabbed a finger at Talia. "You." Her mouth worked, but no words would come. Thirty seconds passed before she turned on her heel and, shaking her head in disgust, walked out the door without looking back.

"Something you need to tell me?" Lottie tapped an impatient foot.

"It was my fault." Shame pinked Talia's cheeks, fluttered her eyelashes down to them when she couldn't face her sister. "I thought if she dropped out, you might ask me."

Lottie looked like she wanted to rip Talia apart until she paused long enough to take in her sister's posture, and the miserable look on her face. "Oh, Tally. How could you let me think so poorly of Sabra for all these years?"

"Didn't know you'd be the champion grudge carrier, did I?"

"We'll talk about this later. In private." Lottie flashed an unreadable look at the captive audience standing around her. "Show's over." Her eyes fell on Allegra, who was currently ignoring Chet's whispered queries about how long she'd been in town. Anyone with eyes could see Allegra had no interest in the man. And, as of that moment, Lottie was done mooning over him. Righting a wrong and repairing a friendship took precedence.

Chapter 17

"Vodka soda, lime; coconut rum and diet; and a sex on the beach!" Mindy barked at the bartender over the din of rock music and shouted conversations. How anyone could work in this atmosphere every evening was beyond her.

The Barnyard was always packed on Friday nights, and with everyone having been cooped up inside due to weather for the past few weeks, it was closing in on maximum capacity. Chloe and Veronica secured a postage stamp sized table in the billiard room while Mindy snaked her tiny frame through the crowd practically unnoticed, claiming a coveted spot at the bar. She was back with their drinks in no time flat.

Divided into three sections situated around a central, circular bar, patrons could choose from live entertainment or karaoke on one side; pool or darts on the other; and an old-school arcade in between.

The Barnyard, a local Gilmore legend, served as a meeting place for several surrounding towns, including Ponderosa Pines. Half the fun was people watching, and they spent a good quarter hour doing just that.

"So, give us the dirt, Chloe." Veronica finally prompted, throwing Mindy a raised eyebrow while Chloe's gaze was diverted to an increasingly competitive game of darts going on in the corner. "We want to know about you and Nate—and don't leave out the gory details."

Chloe met her eyes squarely and replied bluntly, "First tell me why you two never mentioned how close you were to opening the shop. I'm a little hurt, actually, that you didn't tell me." Chloe wrinkled her nose at her friends and flicked a narrow-eyed glare back and forth between them.

Mindy sipped her drink innocently, avoiding direct eye contact and pretending not to have heard the question. It had been Veronica's idea to freeze out Chloe; to "teach her a lesson", and now it was her responsibility to explain.

"We figured what's good for the goose is good for the gander." She stated calmly, keeping her gaze locked onto Chloe's while stirring her drink with a tiny plastic sword.

A moment of panic widened Chloe's eyes. She gulped before venturing, "What are you talking about?"

"We know you're Miss Busybody." Veronica replied coolly. "And we're a bit hurt that *you* didn't tell *us*." Now that the deed had been done, Mindy nodded in agreement.

"I...you...I couldn't..." Chloe sputtered. "I wasn't allowed to tell you. You really think I haven't wanted to?" She couldn't even process the implications of this development. Now at least five people in town knew her secret, and she was on her way to being the worst 'Babble & Spin' author in Ponderosa Pines history.

Mindy reached over and placed a reassuring hand on Chloe's arm, softening at her friend's obvious distress. "Don't worry, Chlo, we would never say anything. And it's only because we know you so well that we figured it out."

"How did you know?"

"A couple of familiar phrases raised our eyebrows, and then we set a trap." Mindy grinned.

"Yeah," Veronica agreed. "Remember that rumor about Summer Daniels going to Portland for a Botox treatment? Totally untrue, but I heard her and Millie Jacobs telling a whole group of their catty little friends that EV's had work done, so we figured she deserved it. You're the only one we told, and lo and behold, it was printed the next week." She finished triumphantly.

"Well, for crying out loud. You have no idea how badly I wanted to tell you! What a relief!" She hopped down from her bar stool and ran over for a group hug before launching into the tale of how she had been recruited by Wesley for the position, and her concern over the repercussions of keeping her friends in the dark. Luckily, it seemed to be working out better than Chloe could have hoped.

Mindy made another trip to the bar, returning with a second round. "To no more secrets!" She toasted. "To no more secrets!"

"Hold the table while I run to the ladies'." Chloe instructed, knees pressed firmly together after procrastinating past the point of comfort. A packed house meant packed bathrooms, and she didn't relish standing in line.

Picking at her cuticles in an attempt to ignore the

mounting urge, Chloe didn't notice when a familiar figure joined the line behind her.

"Oh, hi Chloe. Long time, no see." It was Carrie Burnsoll, whom Chloe remembered fondly as the towheaded little girl who had followed her around like a tail during intermittent visits to the Pines, back when Chloe and her mother lived like nomads and only returned home occasionally.

"Carrie! I knew you were back in town, but I barely recognize you! Aren't you still twelve years old, and where's that Barbie doll you used to cart everywhere?" She laughed, reaching out to give Carrie a friendly hug.

The younger woman rolled her eyes. "I think my dad still has it back in my old room. So how are you doing? Congratulations on your engagement!"

"Thanks." Chloe automatically looked down at the diamond ring on her left hand, remembering the way Nate had looked soulfully into her eyes as he asked her to be his wife. "I think congratulations are going to be in order for your dad pretty soon, too!"

At the mention of Dalton's future with EV, Carrie's eyes clouded and her lips sank into a scowl. "We'll see. After all, it's EV Torrence. She'll be through with him before he has a chance to kneel."

Taken aback at Carrie's obvious distaste for her very best friend, Chloe was rendered speechless—but only for a moment. EV had been right; Chloe was overdue for a blowup. Liquid courage and the high of relief she was still riding after Veronica and Mindy's bombshell prompted a rant poor Carrie hadn't expected.

"You know what, Carrie, you're making a big mistake with that attitude. I was willing to give you the benefit of the doubt, but now you're just spitting vinegar. I don't know if you realize just how lucky you would be to have a stepmother like EV. She's been through hell and back, and you have absolutely no idea what you're talking about. How crushed do you think Dalton was after your mother left? Do you really think he'd get into another relationship if it wasn't going anywhere? I know for a fact that EV loves him, and would die before she hurt him like that! You need a serious reality check; grow up, and stop acting like a spoiled brat!"

Chloe stalked off into the restroom, leaving Carrie gaping after her. *That felt good, though I'll probably regret opening my mouth tomorrow.* She thought, then pushed the encounter from her mind as she made her way back through the crowd to her friends.

"We need to talk." Carrie stepped into EV's kitchen without being invited. She turned to EV with a face set in cold lines of disapproval. "What are your intentions toward my father?"

The question shocked EV so thoroughly she answered without thinking. "I love him. Why? Is that a problem for you?" There was no defensiveness in her tone because EV truly cared about Carrie's feelings on the subject.

"No. Yes. I don't know." Carrie pulled off her puffy winter coat and, making her way toward a sofa by the fireplace, tossed the garment over the back. She perched on the edge of the cushioned seat while EV moved to sit across from her. The air in the room seemed to move a little faster to accommodate the volume of emotion Dalton's daughter was sifting through. "I can't watch him get pounded into the ground again. I don't think he saw it coming when Mom left, and for a little while, he fell apart. That's when he put the coffee shop up for sale and applied to be a cop of all things. At his age."

EV choked back a grin. Fifty-three, to her, felt very little different from twenty-three, but she remembered being Carrie's age and thinking anyone over fifty ancient. There were women her age still having babies. Good grief, what a scandal that would be. Caught up in imagining the look on Lottie's face, EV didn't hear Carrie's question. It was easy enough to figure out, given the path this conversation was taking.

When EV didn't answer quickly enough, Carrie continued. "Old love 'em and leave 'em EV strikes again. Can't settle down because no man is good enough for her highness, the Ice Queen."

"What? No." Surprised at the amount of venom in Carrie's tone, EV took a moment to form an answer that would shock Carrie with its force of truth. "It was the other way around—I wasn't good enough for them." In a series of brutally short sentences, EV laid the bones of her past before Dalton's daughter and hoped for absolution.

"I had no idea." Carrie tried to imagine how she would cope with an abusive relationship and a late-term miscarriage, and came up empty. "Then you're not planning a romp and dump with my dad?"

Frowning at the term, EV's words fell like dust, "Interesting visual." Her mind raced through a multitude of scenarios, none of them ending with her and Dalton happy together if his daughter remained dead set against the relationship. As it always had, concern turned EV defensive and surly.

"I'll walk away if that's what you want." But when the words fell between them, EV realized they weren't true. She levered her tall frame off the chair, speared hands through a sweep of sable hair, and paced—or maybe stomped would be a better word for it—back and forth in the space between the kitchen area and the living room.

"You want me to say I'm sorry for how I've lived my life? Well, it's not going to happen. I don't owe you an apology, and I don't need your forgiveness. Your father is the best person I know, and he's okay with my past." It took this type of confrontation for EV to finally see things as they were. "How dare you condemn me for doing the best I could to deal with what happened? None of it was my fault." A bell should have dinged somewhere, so profound was this admission.

"It wasn't my fault." EV repeated with a sense of wonder at the relief she felt for letting go of self-blame. "I've been a complete idiot." The last of the shell she'd so carefully constructed and maintained fell away, taking her anger with it. Clear-eyed, EV faced Carrie. "I'm not going to walk away, and I hope you can find a way to be happy for your father, and for me."

Carrie's voice sounded choked with emotion, "I'm sorry. I've been a brat because I couldn't bear to see him get hurt again. Neither one of us was prepared when Mom dropped the bomb on our family out of the blue like that. He's such a good man, he handled everything so well, but I knew it must have been harder for him than he let on. It takes courage to try again. For both of you."

"Then we have your blessing?"

"Yes! Yes, of course." Carrie stood to offer EV an embrace, "Welcome to the family."

The next thing that popped out of EV's mouth surprised her almost as much as it did Carrie. "I'm going to marry that man. If he'll have me."

Chapter 18

"Allegra Worth, of all people? I know she's gotten much more pleasant lately, and she looks a lot less like Cruella DeVille than she used to, but the woman still gives me a touch of the heebies." Chloe shook the image of Allegra's gun-wielding husband from her head as EV maneuvered Christine onto the snow-packed dirt road that would deposit them on the offending woman's front lawn.

Months earlier, Ashton Worth threatened to shoot himself—in EV's kitchen, no less—after having murdered the man with whom Allegra had been having an affair. It was by far the biggest scandal since Ponderosa Pines' inception, and Allegra's impropriety hadn't been forgotten. Everyone thought she would move on; after all, Allegra hadn't grown up in the Pines, and now that her husband was in prison, it seemed a fresh start might be in order.

Instead, she surprised everyone by not only hanging around, but by becoming more involved in town events.

EV, always able to see the best in people, had dispensed with any animosity toward the woman. "She's not the first person to ever cheat on her husband—which you know I don't agree with—but it's not fair to blame her for Ashton's actions." Chloe had heard the diatribe several times, and wasn't going to argue the point. Especially not since EV had put forth the suggestion that Allegra might have suffered emotional abuse at the hand of her husband. Something about the changes in her gave EV the tingle.

"I know, I know; it's not even that. She just rubs me the wrong way."

"That's because, unlike you, she doesn't tend to speak her mind unless she's backed into a corner. I think you find her unsettling because she's able to keep her emotions in check, and you can never tell what's going on inside her head." EV shot her friend a knowing look, which was completely ignored.

Chloe muttered under her breath, "Or it's because I expect her to breathe fire at me every time her nostrils flare. And, that I keep wondering whether there's something in her closet made of puppy skin?"

"You remember how well she did setting up for the Yule Ball while we were in Ireland. Give the woman a chance." EV softened at Chloe's chagrined expression. "Relax, I'll do the talking. You just sit there and look pretty." EV hopped down from the truck cab and headed inside, leaving Chloe to shoot dagger-filled looks at her back and trudge along unhappily behind her.

An out of breath Allegra answered the door, clad in stretchy, bright purple workout pants and a white tank, her normally coiffed chin-length bob plastered to her flushed face in sweaty strands. Her raised eyebrow and bewildered expression evidenced how infrequently either of the two women had ever shown up on her doorstep.

"Hello EV, Chloe. What brings you here?"

"We were hoping to talk to you for a few moments; is this a bad time?" EV hedged.

"Come on in, just give me a few minutes to change." She led them into the living room, told them to have a seat, and disappeared down a dark hallway, her voice trailing behind her as Chloe and EV made themselves comfortable. "I've been doing a lot of kickboxing lately. It's too cold and snowy for my daily run, but this I can do inside."

"I know what you mean; I've got a punching bag at home that gets a lot more use during the colder months." EV hollered after her absently while taking in the scene before her.

EV leaned close and whispered to Chloe, "I knew she was getting more involved in knitting group lately, but this is a whole new level of obsession. I can barely get through a scarf, and my stitches are never as neat as these." She fingered the corner of a bright yellow throw with envy in her eyes.

Afghans in all the colors of the rainbow were draped over every piece of furniture, sometimes piled two or three layers high. Stacks of sweaters rested on a chintz armchair in one corner, and a shelf in the other was filled with ream after ream of yarn. Looking through an arched doorway into the dining room, EV could see several clear plastic bins clearly labeled 'scarves', 'mittens', and 'boot socks'.

"I think she's going to stock Veronica and Mindy's entire knitted goods section by herself. The woman has more energy than my kittens. She ought to sell it by the bottle; she'd make a fortune." Chloe couldn't keep the slight hint of admiration from her voice; she tended to get bored with a hobby, enjoying herself but never fully immersing into a single activity.

What furniture could be seen under the burden of knitted goods appeared to be of good quality. It looked like Allegra preferred antique to new—another surprise to Chloe. A series of large-scale photographs—high contrast close-ups—of dandelions gone to seed marched down the hall toward where Allegra had disappeared. Something about their ethereal nature suggested fairies might be hiding among the white-topped seeds.

"Don't you love that chandelier?" Blown glass in bright colors dripped from a series of brushed nickel tubes.

Before EV could answer Allegra returned from her bedroom, moved aside a bundle of perfectly-woven afghan squares, and folded her tall frame onto a padded ottoman. Dark hair once religiously clipped and coifed had grown slightly unruly. Without the constant use of a straightening iron, curls softened the hard planes and angles to make her seem more approachable. Allegra the dragon lady was gone. She looked at EV and Chloe expectantly.

"Can you tell us anything about Stacey

Hawthorne?" EV decided to take the fastest route to point A, and figured Allegra was the type who would appreciate directness.

Without so much as the blink of an eye, Allegra proceeded to explain, "She's my lawyer. For my divorce from Ashton."

It was the first time either of them had heard her speak his name since he had been arrested for murder, and her frankness rendered EV momentarily speechless. "Oh, I'm...sorry about that." She sputtered.

"It is what it is. Anyway, Stacey filed the paperwork a few weeks ago, and the waiting period is still in effect for another month. I haven't spoken to or seen her recently, and I wasn't expecting to until we could proceed with the case. I was living here when all that business in Boston went down; I don't know why you think I'd know any more than you do." Allegra shrugged her shoulders and looked at them both expectantly.

"What business in Boston?" Chloe and EV asked in unison, eyes wide.

"You mean you don't know about Stacey's last big case in Boston? I thought you two would have been all over that like a cheap suit right from the beginning."

EV had half a mind to string Dalton up by his shoelaces, but couldn't help admiring the way the man could keep a secret. "Tell us what you know, Allegra, please." She asked again calmly.

"Stacey worked for the DA's office; you knew that, right? Well, she was involved in a case against Cormack McArney—Big Mac—the notorious Irish mob boss. He had already done time for tax evasion, and hired a public accounting firm to do a set of clean books. When the senior CPA assigned to his case realized there was still something off, he blew the whistle and sent McArney back to prison."

"So that's why Stacey came back to Gilmore? She told you this?"

"No, actually, she never mentioned the case, even when she found out I was from Boston. She didn't even acknowledge she lived there, for that matter. The only reason I know is because my father used to work for a competing accounting firm before he retired. He followed the case religiously, and talked my ear off about it while it was in court. I'm not sure if she was even mentioned in any of the news reports." Allegra paused, allowing Chloe and EV to soak in this new deluge of information before dropping a final word bomb.

"The CPA who testified died a week or so ago—fell off a roof, though that sounds a little fishy to me—and it jogged my memory. I remembered hearing Stacey's name somewhere before, but couldn't place it. I can't help thinking Stacey's attack has something to do with her involvement, but then again, I could be wrong."

EV didn't think so, and neither did Chloe from the look on her face. The decision to focus on Stacey's personal life had seemed like a good one at the time, and EV knew without a doubt that Nate and Dalton had allowed them to fall down the wrong rabbit hole on purpose.

"Allegra," EV asked, "why didn't you say anything about this sooner?"

She shrugged, "You never asked."

Chapter 19

"You didn't ask." Chloe ranted in a fairly close impression of Allegra's broad accent as she and EV headed back to their part of town. "That encounter did nothing to make me like her any better; in fact, I'm more irritated with her now than ever."

EV grudgingly agreed, but still couldn't help liking a woman who had guts enough to face up to scandal without backing down. "It seemed like she thought we already knew, and perhaps she's right—we should have turned over every rock related to Stacey when we first started investigating. It's just as much our fault..."

Chloe crossed her arms petulantly, but knew EV was right. "I think it might be time to have a conversation with Nate and Dalton—share some information. There hasn't been a break in the case; maybe they're missing information that we have, and vice-versa."

"Sure, let me drop off Christine and call Dalton. We'll all meet back at your place." EV replied as she pulled into Chloe's driveway. Minutes later, she came in through Chloe's back door and settled into a cushioned dining room chair. "They're on their way." If the slight smirk didn't tip Chloe off that EV had done something, the glint in her eye should have.

"What's going on?!" Nate bellowed as he and Dalton charged through the front door ten minutes later. Chloe shot a quizzical look at EV.

"I may have used the word 'emergency' in my text. Oops!" EV replied with a wink and no trace of remorse. "We're in here!" She shouted.

Eyes wide, Nate and Dalton rounded the corner, noticed Chloe and EV sitting calmly at the table, and heaved identical heavy sighs.

"I take it you have info for us." Dalton stated with minor annoyance, which was wiped away by the feel of EV's mouth on his. He even managed a smile when he noticed the spread Chloe had put together along with a pitcher of fresh lemonade, all waiting on the kitchen counter. "And lunch. OK, you're off the hook." He said, a chicken salad sandwich already in hand. Chloe handed him a sugar-rimmed glass of the tart beverage, dropping a slice of lemon in at the last second as a garnish. The sun-colored rind whispered of summer days, even if drifts of icy white still blanketed the town.

"I'm sorry for alarming you, but this is important. It's time for a truce, at least temporarily." EV's tone brought Dalton back to earth, and both he and Nate looked at Chloe and EV expectantly.

"Let's start from the beginning. We'll show you ours if you show us yours." She challenged and, accepting Nate and Dalton's twin nods of agreement, continued.

"You know we talked to Rhonda, which led us to Tank, who was a dead end. After that, we decided to go check in with Christian. He mentioned a tall, dark-haired man who visited the hospital." EV went on to explain how Stacey's neighbor had also seen a man skulking around, and why they had come to suspect Wesley.

"I assume you spoke to Wesley also?" Nate said dryly.

"Of course, and he told us about some woman Stacey was trying to protect. Alicia, her name was; he didn't know her last name, but he knew she was involved in some high-profile case Stacey was working on. Our last stop was Allegra—she hired Stacey to handle her divorce—and that's why you're here." EV took a deep breath; it was a lot of information to relay all at once.

Chloe took the opportunity to speak, having been on the edge of her seat the whole time. "Allegra seemed certain this whole thing has to do with the McDonald's case Stacey was working on."

Dalton snorted, and even Nate cracked a smile. "You mean the Cormack McArney 'Big Mac' case?"

"Whatever. Not the point. Allegra said the head accountant who testified against *Big Mac* just died, and she didn't seem to buy the official ruling of 'accident'." Chloe crossed her arms and leaned back in her chair, admiring Nate's handsome face as he processed the information.

Nate turned to Dalton. "Do you remember the name Alicia coming up in that McArney case file? I sure don't."

"Nope, and I went through that monstrosity with a fine-toothed comb. But I think the more pressing question is: was this accountant guy's death really an accident?"

Chloe had already rushed up the stairs and

grabbed her laptop before Dalton could finish his thought, and was booting it up moments later. "Let's see if we can find an obituary. What was his name?"

"Trafton. Ronald Trafton." A few taps of the keys and a couple of clicks later, and bingo.

"It's short. Ronald Trafton, widower, age 58, result of accidental death. No surviving relatives mentioned; that's sad. Let's check media coverage. Here—there's one small story—Ronald Trafton, fell from the roof of a 5-story building, speculation of suicide but ultimately deemed accidental. The building held Levy & Wade's accounting offices, and sources say he was known to take breaks up there from time to time."

"It's been freezing cold outside, and this old man is wandering around on windy rooftops? You're right, that does sound odd." Nate mused. "I wonder why Tim didn't mention this to me when I asked him about the McArney case. Any good detective would be asking more questions than that."

"Great, now I'm getting the tinglies." Dalton rose from his seat and, ignoring EV's snort over the word *tinglies*, began to pace the room.

Everyone was silent, appraising the stony look on Nate's face. When he realized they had all been staring at him for a good 30 seconds he threw his hands in the air in frustration.

"Clearly, there's something we're missing, and I don't think we're going to find it without getting our hands dirty. The weather is supposed to hold for another couple of days, so here's what we're going to do. Dalton and I are going to pack a bag and head down to Boston first thing in the morning. You two are going to agree to a 24-hour detente. I mean it; if the Irish mob is involved, it's way too dangerous for you to be poking around. If you can't agree, you're coming with us, so make your choice." Nate's stern expression and power of authority gave Chloe a whole different type of tinglies.

"All right. All right. You've got a point. And we're not going with you, we have our hands full with WHaC as it is."

After swearing on everything Nate and Dalton could think of—Chloe's engagement ring, EV's collection of tapestries, living parents, and every family heirloom in between—the men finally seemed satisfied, and declared it was way past time for a cigar break. Alone in the tool shed, the two cemented their plans for the morning.

"You know, I can't help but wonder if this Alicia

woman is the mystery number on Stacey's cell phone records." Dalton said thoughtfully. "It would make sense, right?"

"Yeah, too bad it was a burner with a generic voicemail greeting. Just our luck."

Chapter 20

Beep...beep...beep. Christian absentmindedly counted Stacey's heartbeats in his head, the constant rhythm reminding him that she was still there, and could still wake up. He hadn't been more than a few feet from her side in over a week, and he had no intention of leaving until she either came around, or...well, he wasn't willing to think about the alternative.

His sanity rode on her pulling through. But that wasn't the only thing.

"Please," he whispered for about the thousandth time, "please come back. I'll give you anything you could ever want. Or nothing, if that's your choice. I'll walk away if you tell me to, as long as you wake up and keep living your life." With his whole heart, he hoped that if Stacey did wake up, she didn't choose the latter. It was crazy. He knew it was, and yet Christian felt his heart would break if she turned him away. Was it possible to fall in love with a stranger? Or was he simply attached to her because he had saved her life?

He couldn't explain why he was felt the way he did about a person he had never even carried on a reciprocal conversation with, but somewhere deep down Christian knew fate had sent him out that night. He had been meant to help Stacey. Already he had unburdened his soul to her; confided his darkest secrets knowing the chance she could actually hear him was slim.

Christian buried his head in the rumpled sheets at the edge of the bed, silent tears streaming from his eyes and leaving dark blotches on the worn cotton. Something brushed against his hair, so lightly he nearly mistook it for a draft from the overhead air duct before snapping his head up and training his eyes on Stacey's prone figure. For the first time, there was life in her face: her eyes were open, her hand stretched out, reaching for his. He swallowed hard, noted the recognition in her tentative smile, and twined her fingers with his own.

Chapter 21

An hour outside of Boston, the weather app on Dalton's phone signaled an alarm. "The storm tracking up the Atlantic changed course, and now it looks like we're headed right into its path. Blizzard conditions with major snowfall over the next twelve to fourteen hours." His serious expression lightened a bit when he added, "And, it's the storm of the decade. Again."

"Should just call it the storm of the week. How long until it makes landfall?"

Dalton consulted his phone, "Bad news. It's already slamming Nantucket, so it might actually beat us to Boston. Good grief, they've named it Chloe."

That elicited a snort from Nate. "Totally appropriate."

Talk turned to sports until Dalton's phone vibrated again. More dire weather warnings.

By the time Nate turned off Route 1 to pick up the 93 South, visibility was reduced to a point not much past the end of his hood. His eyes felt dry and scratchy from an hour of staring into snow-blown spears of white angling toward him from out of the gray daylight. The wipers were well on the way to having him hypnotized. As tired as he was, he nearly missed the turn after his exit. Walking through the glass doors of the venerable brick building that housed the District 4 precinct after an extra hour in the car, he felt half crippled from tension. Despite the plan to let Dalton take the lead, Nate was the one with the contacts at D-4—his roommate from the Academy had taken a job there a few years back, and, as luck would have it, had worked the Big Mac case in a peripheral way.

Dalton's first impression of Tim McReady was that he was a little cocky in that way that men of shorter stature can be. Dalton could have overlooked that if he hadn't made several pointed comments about Nate's tenure in the boonies. When he couldn't take it anymore, Dalton interjected that Ponderosa Pines was only boonies adjacent and Tim seemed stymied for a comeback to that comment.

Nate's face betrayed nothing as he listened to Tim

brag about how he had been the one to break the case wide open while Dalton's developing cop sense sent up fireworks for signals. During the hour they spoke, the man contradicted himself several times. Beyond that, something about Tim seemed off and by the way he talked, he was unaware that Nate and Dalton already had access to the relevant case files.

"What can you tell me about someone named Alicia who is related to the case?" Dalton pried. She was the reason they had traveled all this way, and his gut insisted she was the key to what had happened to Stacey.

Tim scoffed, "She was a nobody. Just some flunky who took off before the trial. She wasn't even on the witness list. Why would you waste your time looking at her?" His tone implied that he was dealing with idiots.

"It's a loose end."

"Trust me, she's tied." Tim crossed his arms over his chest and fixed squinted eyes on Dalton's face, "too bad about that accountant, the guy who testified —falling off a roof like that."

When it seemed that Tim had told them everything he knew, Dalton reminded Nate that they had another stop to make that afternoon.

"Sure is a shame what happened to that Hawthorne woman. I hear her odds drop every day she's in a coma." Sympathy so false it was thinner than tissue paper put the final nail in Tim's coffin when it came to Dalton having any sort of respect for the man.

"Miracles happen every day," was all he said, other than a terse goodbye. The walk to the car was silent, but the minute the door thunked closed behind him, Dalton exploded. "I hate to say it but your friend is either crooked or dumber than a bag of doorknobs. Or am I just reading into things?"

Nate's grim expression was all the answer Dalton needed. "We did learn something," Nate pointed out. "Alicia disappeared of her own free will, not into witness protection. I'm thinking she had help."

"From Stacey. And following that logic, it was Alicia she called that night. The mystery burner phone with the canned outgoing message."

"Whole thing would be over and done if we had a name to go with that number." Nate smacked the steering wheel with the palm of his hand.

"Not quite, we have theories about certain organizations, but we still haven't pinned down a suspect."

The next two hours would solve both those mysteries and create a new problem.

The building that housed Levy & Wade boasted three floors of gleaming chrome and glass decor straight out of the seventies, complete with chairs clad in faux leather. Behind the raised reception area, walls of glass soared on all three sides to create the illusion of an open floor plan. Even the elevator was made out of glass. "Am I having a flashback?" Dalton wondered. "Never mind, you weren't even born when this was in style.

"According to Chloe, everything comes back around eventually."

"Like the way a stopped clock is right twice a day?"

"I guess." The metaphor almost made sense to Nate.

A plump woman in her late sixties manned the reception desk with all the finesse of an armed guard dog. She made no effort to preserve the privacy of whoever was on the other end of the phone currently tucked between her shoulder and ear. No pesky, updated technology such as a headset here. A single finger raised when Nate and Dalton approached, and it took about the same amount of time as an eye blink to figure out she had her finger firmly planted on the pulse of the business. In investigating any case, Nate knew there were levels of information to be plumbed. The basics could be found in any well-constructed case file: interviews with the key players, criminal history, background. But the best way to get the true dirt was to talk to the people who spent their days watching, largely ignored, from the sidelines. The problem with this particular group was knowing which side they were on.

Alicia and Ronald had come down heavily on the side of good, and look where it had gotten them. Ronald was dead, and Alicia had been in the wind for a long time.

Trudy, the receptionist, dropped the phone back into its cradle with a firm click. "Can I help you with something?"

After introductions were complete, Dalton explained the reason for their visit.

"Anything you could tell us about Alicia would help. We only want to protect her." He stood firm under the piercing stare of her Eagle eye. Trudy reminded him of his fifth-grade teacher; the one who could spot a lie from fifty paces.

"I believe you, but I'm afraid I can't help you."

Trudy, choosing her words carefully, put a slight emphasis on the word can't. Nate caught the motion when her eyes flickered toward a set of offices on the third floor, then back to her phone which, being old-fashioned, had an intercom built in. A red light blinked. Nate took the hint.

"Could you show us where she used to work? It might help us get a better sense of her."

"Of course, but you know she hasn't worked here in months."

Nate nodded, and Trudy tapped a button the phone; presumably the one that would route phone calls elsewhere in her absence.

"Follow me, please." Once out of sight or hearing from the front desk, Trudy spoke in a rushed manner, "Alicia is in trouble. They're saying she's the one who was working with Big Mac, and I know better. Ronald is dead because the evidence kept building against him, even though he was the one who testified for the prosecution. It's all a ploy to get a criminal out of jail, and I'm afraid my boss is in on it."

Passing through the hallway, Dalton happened to glance at a line of photographs depicting a company celebration. One face caught his eye. "Nate, look." He stopped and pointed to the smiling face of the woman he knew as Jessamyn Sanders. Half the puzzle locked into place. Still, they let Trudy lead them to a small cubicle where after a cursory look around, Nate said, "Thank you, Trudy. I believe we've seen enough."

During the tense drive north, the conversation centered on what to do next. With Alicia's identity providing a firm link to Stacey, the question of her attacker was the final hurdle. Trudy had just given them motive for someone wanting to find Jessamyn, and it wasn't a huge leap to consider Stacey as the conduit for making that happen.

With the weather holding at near white-out conditions, roads were being closed all over the tri-state area. They took side streets as far as Chelsea before Nate made the executive decision to find a hotel for the night. Better a warm bed than a cold car, and in the morning, they could hit Route 1 north to the Maine Turnpike.

It took three tries to find a vacancy; Nate hadn't been the only one with common sense enough to hunker down and wait out the storm—and they would be doing so crammed into a single room in the seediest hotel this side of the city limits. The only saving graces were cable TV and a pair of twin beds.

Not even for safety's sake did the idea of sharing a bed sound appealing.

Since Chloe and EV were too far away to lecture on the lack of dietary merit to be found in takeout burgers, Dalton went back out for drive-through.

"Bacon, cheddar, and tater tots. I believe that covers all the basic food groups. Potato is a vegetable, right? There's tomato on the burgers anyhow." He spread the empty bag out on the table, thinking it might be the cleaner option of the two surfaces. "We got any sports channels?"

"Sorry, looks like the free cable is mostly local channels." Nate's posture changed when he flipped past something that caught his eye, then clicked back. "Look at that, it's some kind of extended coverage of the Big Mac trial." He boosted the volume to listen to the newscaster talk about how the tragic death of Ronald—the man Big Mac insisted had been behind the fuzzy bookkeeping that jailed him—had brought the story back into the limelight.

A few minutes into the footage, Dalton waved a cheese-dripping tot at the screen. "Did you see that? Is that Wesley?"

Nate squinted at the screen, "Looks like him from

the back. Come on, turn around....turn around...that's right...turn."

"That's not Wesley." Dalton's stomach dropped. "That's Chet Morgan." Forgetting he still held the greasy tot, he slapped his forehead. "We've got to warn the girls. Morgan's dangerous."

Already a step ahead of him, Nate hit speed dial on his phone. "It's going straight to voice mail without even ringing first. Either her battery died, or she's out of area. I'll try the home phone." Face grave, Nate quoted the recorded message. "All circuits are currently busy."

"How are we going to warn them if the storm's knocked out phone access? I've got a bad feeling about all this." Dalton pulled up the travel advisory site for the state. "The 'pike's still closed, which means the secondary roads are even worse. Weather app says we've got another twelve hours of heavy snowfall before the tail end passes over us, and a few more after that before it clears the Pines. And you know Gilmore won't send a plow out on the side roads between the two towns until everything else is cleared." Bitterness quirked his lips.

Nate pinched the bridge of his nose between his thumb and index finger. Nothing seemed likely to stop the throb of tension induced headache. "We're looking at a minimum of 24 hours with drive time, maybe more."

"Times like these are when jetpacks would come in handy. Weren't we supposed to have flying cars by now?" George Jetson would be so ashamed.

"Let me make a call. It's a long shot, but worth a try if I can get through to Javi. He did mention something about travel not being a problem if I took that job." Nate pulled up the number and made the call.

Chapter 22

The only person in the world able to flap the normally unflappable Priscilla Lewellyn was EV Torrence. All it took was half a minute of watching EV attempt a new knitting pattern and Priscilla was poised to dive off the deep end.

"What are you doing? It's a simple cable. Four stitches crossed over from right to left. Keep the cable needle in front of the work." Priscilla pulled the needles forcefully from EV's hands while EV suppressed a smirk. It wasn't that she enjoyed getting the yarn guru all riled up, but EV had just never managed to find the knitting zen everyone else seemed to fall into with ease.

It wasn't that EV had two left thumbs—she could pull apart all the fiddly bits in Christine's carburetor and have it back to working in no time. There was a logic and method to mechanical items she understood on a gut level. Knitting should have been the same; a series of repeated movements producing similar results. It never seemed to work that way for her. EV found it impossible to relax into the rhythm, so instead of providing a sense of serenity, the whole process made her cranky. If not for the social aspect of the group, she would have done Priscilla a favor and quit long ago.

Or maybe not, given the amount of non-knitting activity accomplished in the little room behind Thread. Nestled into the middle of what was laughingly called the business area of Ponderosa Pines, the fabric shop occupied a narrow, but deep section of the five adjoining shops making up the north side of the street. The back room contained a cast-off sofa and several armchairs. For those rare times when overflow required more seating, Priscilla had a stack of folding chairs in a small closet in the back. To make the room even cozier, she'd hung cheerfully patterned quilts on every wall. At least twice a week during the winter, and once a week during the summer, the small group met to knit, and to gossip, and to plan. Officially, all town activities must be channeled through the elders and elected leaders. Unofficially, these women handled almost all of the thousands of details involved with planning any one of several yearly town festivals.

Since Priscilla had taken away her pathetic excuse of a sample square, EV had time to look around the room and gauge the emotional status of the group. Lottie and Talia appeared to be fully entrenched in the silent treatment phase of their latest battle. Each sister pointedly ignored the other except for a series of exaggerated eye rolls. Whether or not this was an extension of the most recent airing of their dirty laundry or another fight entirely, their attitudes toward each other were normal for them.

EV suspected their constant bickering was the reason the group had begun to shrink as soon as Lottie became a regular member. Maybe when some of the snowbirds came back from whatever warm climes they chose to roost in for the winter, the numbers would increase again.

Allegra sat in her usual spot; curious eyes taking in everything around her while offering very little in the way of discussion on the topic at hand—which, of course, centered around two matters: Stacey

Hawthorne and what was being done to find her attempted killer, and the extended absence of Jessamyn Sanders from the group.

"Nate and Dalton are following a lead in Boston, and we've promised not to meddle while they're gone." Chloe's matter of fact tone discouraged any further inquiry on that subject, which left Jessamyn's burgeoning relationship with Tank Daniels open for speculation.

"Do you think they're shacking up?" Talia lowered her voice to a scandalized whisper.

"Oh, for Pete's sake, are you eighty? No one uses that phrase anymore." Lottie broke the silence between them.

Before another spat could form, Priscilla commented, "I think they make a lovely couple."

Exiting Thread, knitting bag slung over her shoulder, a bright light and a flurry of activity across the street caught Chloe's attention. It was coming from the old schoolhouse, and she could see Veronica's silhouette gesticulating wildly inside.

"Let's pop over and see how the girls are doing." Chloe dragged EV along behind her and entered the shop, the old, rheumatic door swinging noisily shut behind them.

Veronica sidled up to the pair and gave them each a quick hug. "Hey, Sweets, what's going on?"

"We saw you from across the street and wanted to check it out." Chloe looked around appreciatively. "This is incredible; you two just started a few days ago! How did you get this much finished so quickly?"

Dozens of empty shelves lined the walls of the almost too-large space, but it was obvious that after some creative placement the room would be divided off into sections. Box after box of merchandise rested in the rear right corner, among which EV spotted the bins of knit accessories she had seen at Allegra's house. The walls, a lovely shade of blue gray, complimented the mottled gold of the pressed tin ceilings, and transformed the once-cavernous room into something warm and cozy.

"By haranguing Jace and Franklin into helping. Jace tapped his kickball buddies, and Franklin made the kids come help. They laid the floor, painted, and hung all these shelves in two days, and then carted in all of our furniture and merchandise. We've still got some setting up and decorating to do, and of course the yoga studio won't be completed for another few weeks." She rolled her eyes toward the second floor. "We've got climate control issues upstairs, and are just waiting on Tank to draw up plans and install the new system."

"Amazing," EV breathed. "I've seen this building go through a lot of changes during my life, and I've got to say, this is the most fun. You know I went to school here many moons ago. There were only ten of us kids spanning kindergarten through fourth grade, and we were all taught in the same room by the same teacher. It was such a shame to see this space going empty for so long." She looked around nostalgically. "You've done a wonderful job converting it. I can't wait to shop!"

Mindy grinned widely in appreciation of the compliment, and Veronica hugged EV once more before springing off to move some clothing racks into position.

"I second that!" Chloe agreed enthusiastically, left her knitting bag in a heap by the checkout counter, and began sifting curiously through a couple of boxes of merchandise with absolutely zero shame.

"We haven't gone through that box yet, so who knows what's in there." Veronica's warning came about two seconds too late as Chloe pulled out a bundle of men's clothing that might have been dipped in a vat of cologne so old it conjured images of middle school dances.

Chloe covered her mouth to cough, then caught another whiff of the stuff clinging to her fingers, which triggered another emanation that was half cough, half sneeze. Veronica couldn't help but let a giggle escape her lips.

"Told you. There's some hand sani in my purse by the register, if you can find it."

Digging through the many pockets of Veronica's handbag, Chloe deposited several odd items onto the glass checkout counter: a couple of lint-covered earplugs; a pair of pliers; and a bra. In another, deeper section Chloe's hand struck something odd that she couldn't quite place. It felt both hard and crumbly at the same time. Pulling out a plastic bag full of rice, she noticed a cell phone buried in it.

"This isn't your phone, V." Chloe held the bag above her head for Veronica to see.

"Oh, I forgot that was in there. It fell out of someone's pocket that day Harley played snow-mo-bowling for tourists. Plug it in and see if it turns on; maybe we can figure out who the owner is."

EV leaned against the opposite side of the counter and watched as Chloe powered on the device. After a few seconds the home screen popped up, and her fingers flew over the keys to open the recent call log.

"The last call was to 'Alicia'!" EV exclaimed while Chloe's jaw hung open in astonishment.

"Maybe it's a coincidence. Let's see what other numbers were called." Chloe mused, recovering her composure. "Oh, my goodness, the next outgoing call is to 'Wesley' and then there are at least a dozen calls to and from Steinke, Burns, and Pruitt. Are you thinking what I'm thinking?"

"If you're thinking that this is Stacey Hawthorne's missing phone, then yes." EV circled the counter to get a better look at the screen. "Look at the dates and times; those last two calls were made right about the time of her accident!" Chloe handed her the phone, and EV's eyes lit upon the number displayed below Alicia's name.

"Wait a second, I know that number. At least I think I do." EV's face scrunched up in thought as she mentally sifted through the dozens of numbers stored in her brain.

"Oh, hell, hang on, I've got to know, or it will drive me crazy," she said after a moment, and jogged over to where her purse lay open on the floor. "Let's call it and see."

EV tapped a few keys and hit the 'Send' key. As soon as she did, her incredibly smart phone recognized the number as a stored contact, and Alicia's new name popped up on the screen.

"Holy Moses, Alicia isn't going by Alicia anymore. She's Jessamyn Sanders!"

Chapter 23

Before they could say another word, David Erickson burst through the door with a look of panicked wonder on his face. "EV, I thought I saw you headed over here. Can you come? Rhonda's water broke and she's freaking out." Without thinking, EV tapped the 'End Call' button on her phone before Jessamyn—or Alicia—could answer, all thoughts besides 'there's a baby on the way' pushed aside for the moment.

A short moment.

Why me? Can't anyone do anything in this town unless I'm there to watch? EV's thoughts had less to do with pique than with being slightly squeamish when it came to anything of a medical nature. There was a very good reason why she had no interest in owning farm animals. Still, she knew she would go. But not alone. Veronica had been through this five times—if anyone was qualified to help Rhonda, it would be her.

"Go back to her, we'll be right there." Her reassurance and a gentle squeeze of his arm calmed David down from a state six steps above frantic to one of mild panic. With a nod of relief, he rushed back out into the slanting white snowstorm.

"She couldn't have chosen a less convenient time to go into labor; this storm is worse than the last one." EV dusted off her hands and took a moment to think about the best course of action. "We're all going to go see what we can do to help. Mindy, how far along are you in your doula training?"

"Far enough to be helpful, not far enough to handle a birth on my own unless there's no other option, and then I guess I could muddle through it if I had to." It was an honest appraisal.

EV rubbed her forehead but saw no means of escape that wouldn't brand her a coward. "Okay, ladies. Shall we?" Her gaze included Chloe, who would have liked nothing more than to throw open the door and make a run for it—the only thing stopping her was that EV was her ride home. "You too, Ms. Chickenheart. If I have to do this, so do you."

Squeamishness was one more thing the pair of them had in common.

The buildings on the other side of the street were barely visible through the drifting white, and the four of them were so covered in snow they looked like Frosty's harem by the time they blew into the coffee shop. EV noted with surprise that the place was packed, but it would have been hypocritical to make anything more than a mental comment on why people weren't home where they belonged on a day like this.

"They're upstairs." Lottie manned the counter. "Dear Mr. Morgan drove me in by snowmobile so I could help out." EV suppressed a snort. She'd seen Lottie ride that Arctic Cat like a fiend to successfully win several local races. Clearly, playing the fluttery, helpless female was part of her plan to land Chet Morgan. If it worked, he'd be in for a big surprise when her true colors began to shine through.

Shrugging off the kind of thoughts about Lottie's love life that were just too icky to imagine, EV led her damp troop upstairs where David met the lot of them with immense relief. "Rhonda's folks are stuck out at our place and she really wants her mom."

"What about Doc Talbot?" Chloe paled when a low moan issued from the bedroom.

"He's out at Tank's place. The vet couldn't make it over there in the storm, so Doc went out to see if he could help with an early foal and got snowed in. There were four-foot drifts across the road and the big plow hasn't made it over that far, so Jessamyn's bringing him on Tank's Ski-Doo."

"They're not going to try coming across at the narrows, are they? It's too easy to miss that bridge in low visibility," EV chimed in. The last thing they needed was to have more people in danger.

"No, they're taking the loop trail to avoid getting caught in the drifts out on the flats, but it's a lot longer, so it will take a while."

Another moan, this one louder than before, echoed through the small apartment. "David Erickson, you get in here and help me breathe." Rhonda's voice sounded strained. David's expression notched up two more levels of panic. If his eyes got any bigger, they were going to fall out of his head. He grabbed EV by the hand. "You have to help. Please. It's all going too fast and I'm afraid Doc won't make it in time. I can't deliver this baby. I just can't."

"Calm down, David," EV ordered. "We're going to

help." To Mindy, she said, "Let's go take a look. I'm sure there's plenty of time." That turned out to be wishful thinking.

"I'll go boil some water. And gather towels." Anything, Chloe thought, to keep from having to go into that bedroom.

"Okay, Annie Oakley, but I think just the towels will be enough," Veronica teased.

"No hot water? They always get some in the movies, I wondered what they did with it."

"Probably used it to sterilize the knife." When Chloe's face blanched even more, Veronica sent her down to the coffee shop for a cup full of ice chips. Rhonda would welcome the cool moisture in the hours to come. Then she scanned the cozy room for something soft to wrap around the baby when it came. If worse came to worse, with Priscilla right downstairs, she could grab the key and raid Thread for supplies.

In the bedroom, Rhonda panted through the pain. "Hee-hee-hoo. Hee-hee-hoo." Sweat dripped from her hair while gooseflesh covered her body. "How can I be so hot and so cold at the same time?"

"That's part of the miracle. You're doing fine." Mindy spoke in soothing tones. "Did you have a birth plan in place?" She asked David as she helped Rhonda swing her feet over the side of the bed. "We're just going to walk around a little. It will help the baby move into position."

"Is something wrong? He's not breach, is he?" David's voice rose.

"He's fine, and she's dilating well, but the movement will help."

The minute Chloe popped her head back into the shop, a dozen questions hit her in the face.

"Rhonda is in good hands. Doc Talbot is on his way in from Tank's farm," her answers covered most of them.

She looked around the room to see that the place was chock full of customers. Too preoccupied, she had missed seeing so many familiar faces on her way through. While Lottie brewed coffee, Priscilla had donned an apron and was bustling around serving and clearing tables. The surprise of the day was seeing Allegra Worth cheerfully turning out sandwiches in the kitchen with almost military precision. And smiling while she did. The fleeting thought that she looked happy slid through Chloe's mind before being driven out by another.

"Who's running the inn?" Lottie wouldn't leave paying guests.

"Almost everyone left yesterday. There's only Chet and another couple left. I sent them over to Sabra's for the duration."

It seemed a detente had been reached, the second in as many days.

The rush of initial panic subsided to leave Chloe's mind clear.

Half a dozen snowmobiles lined the street in front of The Mudbucket. All around the room, thermal suits draped various surfaces. Several hung on a coat rack by the door; more lay over the backs of their owner's chairs. Seeing them gave Chloe an idea, and Horis was just the man to carry it out.

"Rhonda's folks are stuck at her place across town and she really needs her mom." Chloe let her voice carry across the room, but it was Horis to whom she addressed her comments. "I need a couple volunteers to ride out and get them. A couple more to lend snowsuits in case they're not prepared."

Horis took the hint. "I'll take care of it."

"Okay, great. I'll come back down and keep you all posted." Chloe collected her cup of ice chips and disappeared back upstairs. Her steps only faltered once when she heard a low scream followed by panting breaths. No one was left in the front room, which meant she would have to take the ice chips in to Rhonda herself. Every cell in Chloe's body screamed run. Now. Fast.

Get hold of yourself, you big chicken. She squared her shoulders and stepped through the door.

Flanked by EV on one side, David on the other, Rhonda completed a circuit of the confined space while Mindy encouraged her to keep going. In the far corner of the room, Veronica was talking to someone on her phone. Chloe handed the cup of ice to EV, and quirked an eyebrow at Mindy, who gave her the thumbs up. This wasn't so bad. Nothing too scary seemed to be happening. What she had expected, Chloe wasn't even sure. Blood—maybe some gore. So far, there was nothing more than a panting woman and the smell of something in the air. Rhonda had calmed and was even laughing a little between contractions.

"We'll have quite a story to tell this little guy when he's older." Rhonda winced at a residual bit of cramping.

"How's it going?" Chloe looked at Mindy.

"She's doing great. It won't be long, I think this one is going to set a record for speeding through labor for a first baby."

"Three weeks late and then all in a rush," Rhonda pulled her arm from David's gentle grasp to cradle her belly. "I just wish my mom was here."

"That's what took me so long downstairs," Chloe said, "I put Horis in charge of retrieving your parents." The sound of snowmobiles roaring away came faintly through the front window. "That will be him now. It's a straight shot if they stick to the roads and not the trails. There won't be huge drifts like out toward Tank's place. Any word on Doc Talbot?"

"That's what I was just doing." Veronica said. "I called everyone who lives close enough to the loop trail to hear the sled when it passes by. I've managed to track them as far as Bert and Celia's. They went through there about five minutes ago so they should be here any second now."

Rhonda groaned and stumbled when another contraction hit, her face contorted in pain and she grabbed for David's hand; gripped it so tight Chloe could hear the bones grind together.

"They're getting stronger," David winced and his voice shook a little. "Horis needs to hurry if he's going to make it back with her parents in time." When Rhonda let go of his hand, he leaned away to shake the pain out of it where she couldn't see. A broken hand was little enough price to pay for any comfort his wife might gain from the contact.

"Let's get her back on the bed, I'll need to check her progress just in case Doc doesn't get here soon."

That was Chloe's cue to disappear. Before she had fully made the decision to go, her feet had carried her halfway to the stairs. What on earth was she going to do when it was her time? Drugs. Lots and lots of drugs.

"Chloe." EV's voice called her back before she could escape. Chloe looked back to see EV standing in the doorway of the bedroom holding her cell phone. "You need to take my place. Christian has been trying to call me from the hospital and I need to see what's going on."

"Veronica..." Chloe tried to pass the buck.

"Doesn't know Rhonda as well as we do. Go." EV ignored Chloe's attempt to strike her dead with only the power of her gaze.

"Fine." Her stomach jumped when a cloud of butterflies flared to life in there. "I could have called Christian back," she muttered, but she sucked it up and went toward the bedroom. If Rhonda could push a baby out, the least Chloe could do was hold her hand.

She was completely unprepared for the sight of the baby crowning. It was the most disgusting and the most beautiful thing she'd ever seen. "Oh Rhonda, you're missing this." Chloe looked around frantically. Behind the door she found a full-length mirror and wrestled it into place so Rhonda could watch.

Everything shifted into high gear at that moment. Doc Talbot arrived and calmly took Mindy's place. Horis and his crew got Rhonda's parents there just in time to see the baby being ushered into the world by caring hands. Chloe had a front row seat while keeping the mirror angled for Rhonda to see.

When Doc Talbot pulled out a pair of scissors to cut the cord, Chloe decided she'd seen about all she could handle for one day. "I think you could use some privacy, I'll just be going now." The mirror went back behind the door and she escaped with relief.

EV was nowhere in sight so Chloe went down to give the good news to those waiting in the shop.

"He's here. Mother and son are both doing fine."

"How much did he weigh?" Lottie wanted to know.

"No clue. Why? Is there a pool going?" There probably was. "Where's EV?" Chloe looked around with the niggling feeling someone else was missing.

"She was here a few minutes ago." At some point, Veronica, feeling superfluous, had come downstairs to indulge in a cup of tea. "She was sitting back there," a thumb indicated the far corner of the room, "When Jessamyn came in with Doc Talbot. Jessamyn wouldn't even stop to get warm, she headed right back out to help Tank at the farm. Then, about two minutes later, that Wesley wannabe left. And then EV left."

"Wesley wannabe?" Sometimes talking to Veronica required a decoder ring.

"Yeah, you know, that reporter. The one Lottie's been hot to trot for. Didn't you notice he looks a lot like Wesley? Especially from behind. He can't be very good dating material, though. He just rode off on Lottie's snow machine without her. What a jerk."

The pieces fell into place. Chloe's heart jumped

into her throat. "Do you have your phone? Call Nate and keep trying until you get him. It looks like the snow is finally starting to let up a little. Maybe you'll be able to get through."

She would have killed EV for leaving without her if the other woman hadn't picked that moment to pull old Christine up in front of The Mudbucket. Chloe grabbed her coat, shrugged it on while telling Veronica, "Tell Nate that Jessamyn is Alicia. He'll know what it means."

"Is she in trouble?" Horis asked. He was already pulling the top of his snowmobile suit back on.

"Yeah, she is."

"And you're going after her?" The question was rhetorical. "Not without me. I'll get a couple of the boys together. We'll take the shortcut and meet you there."

"What about the narrows bridge?"

"I've been riding around here for a lot longer than Jessamyn. I could hit that bridge in my sleep. Trust me, we'll be fine."

Chloe raced to jump into the truck with EV.

"It's Chet Morgan."

"Jessamyn's in trouble." They both spoke at the same time.

"I'll call Tank. Horis is going across the narrows. He'll meet us there. You think Morgan has a gun?"

"Maybe, but I know Tank has one." EV's face was grim. "This is going to be a wild ride, but I trust Christine to plow through the drifts as long as we get up a good head of steam first." EV revved up the engine and fishtailed into the first turn.

"According to Veronica, Jess had a two minute head start. Would she have recognized him?"

"I don't know, maybe. Stacey's awake, though. That's what Christian was calling about." Face set in concentration, EV pulled every bit of power she could out of the old truck as the first tall drift came into view. Nearly level with her hood, the packed snow could stop her forward momentum if she didn't hit it hard enough to plow right through.

"Hold on." Four-wheel low provided plenty of power. Christine hit the semi-solid wall of snow with a lurch that sent a white cloud over the truck. Reaching out, EV hit the lever to crank the wipers up to full speed. When the windshield cleared, she could see that they'd made it through the first hurdle. She kept her foot on the gas and barreled toward the next one. Her concentration was so focused, she didn't hear Chloe speaking to Tank in a low voice.

"Tank's not there."

"What do you mean he's not there? Where is he?"

"Abe Zellner's. The foal and mare were doing fine so he snowshoed over to check on Mr. Zellner. He's headed back now."

"Drift!" EV shouted. Chloe braced herself for the thump. Christine hit the bank, then lurched to a stop.

"Too slow. I'll have to back up and try again." As she said it, EV was already jamming the clutch and dropping the shifter into reverse. Several seconds passed while the tires spun. "Easy girl. You can do it." She eased off the gas until the wheels caught. A second run at the drift did the trick.

During the hour spent with the Ericksons, the leading edge of the storm had traveled well beyond the tiny town. Now, only a few bursts of flakes swirled through the darkening sky.

Abe Zellner's house was lit up like a torch, while Tank's place remained relatively dark. Only the barn glowed with light.

"I'm going to cut the headlights. Might buy us a little time if we didn't manage to get ahead of them."

Before she could follow suit, a dark form lurched into the road ahead of them, and EV hit the brakes to rock Christine to a stop mere inches from Tank's familiar form.

"Get in," Chloe cranked her window down to issue the order while Tank hit the quick release clips on his snowshoes. He chucked them into the bed of the truck and climbed in beside Chloe.

"Pull down past the house and park on the other side of the barn."

EV hit the switch to cut off the headlights—not that Christine was the quietest of trucks, so full stealth mode was out of the question, but every little bit helped.

"Let me get this straight. Jessamyn is on the run from a mob hitman because she discovered something funky while doing accounting work for one of their legit businesses?"

"And her former boss is already dead." Moving slower now that the lights were off, most of EV's concentration was focused on driving.

"That's why Stacey was attacked. Right here, turn now." Tank said. "Hurry up. She's coming up the trail, I can see her headlights. She's going to head for the barn because that's where she thinks I'll be. We need to get there first."

"Tank, where are you?" Jessamyn flew through

the door on a dead run. "Someone's trying to kill me. There's so much I haven't told you."

Catching her in his arms for a moment of comfort, Tank said, "I know. It's okay. EV's here with Chloe, they gave me the Reader's Digest version. You'll tell me the rest when this is all over. How much time do we have?"

"Couple minutes, maybe a little less. Looked like he was driving Lottie's Cat and it's no good at breaking trail. I lost him in the potato fields because he kept bogging down."

A gentle kiss was all he had time to give her before pulling her back into the shadowed darkness where EV and Chloe waited. The sound of a single sled droned outside; he was coming in hot, but they had a little time.

"Horis is on the way with reinforcements." EV told Tank.

"Beg to differ," Horis' voice rose from the other side of barn. "I've got Wesley and Willow with me. I told you I could hit that bridge in my sleep; we beat you by three minutes."

"There's not a lot of time to set anything up, so we'll have to play it by ear," EV said.

"I've got a recording app on my phone," Chloe

scanned the place to find the perfect spot. Breaking cover, she tucked her phone into the V created by a short support strut that angled from an upright beam holding the leading edge of the loft above their heads. "If we can get him to confess to Stacey's attack, Nate might just forgive me for coming here. But that means you're going to have to be the one to get him to talk," she turned to Jessamyn, "are you up for it...and do you want us to keep calling you Jessamyn, or would you prefer Alicia?"

"Jessamyn," she answered without hesitation. "Alicia is gone, and I'm finally going to get a chance to do something about it."

"We've got about a minute to get ready, then. Anyone bring a gun?" Chloe's question received the answer she expected. Most Pines residents carried rifles during hunting season, but not during the dead of winter. Except for Abe Zellner, who never left the house without the pistol he wore in a holster under his left arm. His concealed carry permit ranked highly among his prized possessions. Right up there with his collection of Coleman lanterns.

"Grab anything that's handy." Tank ordered, "And hurry."

"Gotta love a barn—best place to find weapons."

EV selected a short hatchet from a wall of tools hanging off pegs. Hefting it, she determined it would throw well enough in a pinch. As an afterthought, she picked up an old window weight that still had a sturdy hank of rope hanging from it. "What's your poison?" She asked Chloe, who cocked an ear to gauge how much longer before Chet burst through the door before choosing a lariat that hung, coiled, from one of the other support beams. "Really?"

"Hey, I've got skills you haven't even seen yet." The two women parted as Chloe took her spot behind the huge rear wheel of an old John Deere tractor. EV, as always, preferring a bird's eye view, slithered up the ladder to the haymow and slid into the shadow created by two adjacent piles of hay.

Quiet fell both inside and outside the barn. Chet Morgan had arrived.

The creaking of the door sent a shiver up Jessamyn's spine just ahead of what felt like liquid steel. Running once had been prudent, but now she would stand.

"Hello Alicia." His voice had lost the jovial tone he'd been using all over town.

"Mr. Morgan. What brings you out this way. And in such bad weather."

"I think you know why I'm here. I've come for you, Alicia." Cold words meant to menace only ticked her off. Furious, she cocked a hip, folded her arms, and lifted her chin defiantly while she appraised him.

"What could you possibly hope to accomplish by killing me?"

"Stupid woman. No one wants to kill you. I've been sent to take you back to Boston where you can clear Levy's name and tell the courts Trafton was the one who cooked the books."

"I don't understand." But it made a certain amount of sense when she thought about it. If Levy worked for the mob, this probably wasn't the first time he had indulged in a bout of fuzzy accounting. When he had failed to pin the blame on her, Ronald had been next in line to become the scapegoat.

"He needed to get his house in order if he wanted to work with the new boss of the organization."

"And who might that be? Quarter Pounder?"

Morgan took a step closer. "You're going to leave with me, now. But don't worry, your new boyfriend won't be lonely for long. I'll take care of him soon enough. It'll look like he was the victim of a home invasion." Chet Morgan lifted his gun to gesture that Jessamyn should move toward the door when a whooping noise sounded over his head. Distracted, he looked up to find the source of the sound, and all hell broke loose.

"Get down," Tank yelled, and leapt to cover Jessamyn's body as she dropped to the floor. EV let go of the window weight she'd been whirling over her head. In the semi-darkness of the barn, the only part of the rusty metal projectile that was visible was the white rope trailing along behind it. Her aim was a little off. Instead of beaning him in the head, it caught Morgan square in the chest and knocked him back two steps.

In reflex, he aimed the gun toward where the weight had come from and got off a single shot before several things happened in rapid succession. Chloe's lariat swooped in and dropped over him to pin his arms to his sides. The shovel Horis swung knocked the gun out of Morgan's hand, and Willow and Wesley tackled him from two different directions at once. Morgan went down in a welter of flailing fists. But the most surprising of all was when Nate slammed through the door, service weapon leveled and Dalton hard on his heels.

"Police, drop your weapon." Two seconds earlier

and they might have had more to do than cuff the barely-conscious man.

"You're a bit late for that, Hoss," Horis drawled, "he's already down."

Nate and Chloe spoke at once.

"Everyone okay?"

"How did you get here?

"Helicopter. Javier." Nate's eyes searched her for signs of injury.

"I think so." Chloe replied to his earlier question. Her ears were still ringing from the sound of the gunshot in the confined area, and her heart felt like it might never slow down again. Tank and Jessamyn stood off to one side, his arms wrapped tightly around her. Horis and his crew had the odd bruise or two, but seemed okay. The only person she couldn't see was EV.

"Where is EV?" Dalton had also picked up on her absence.

Chloe's face went chalk white as she raced for the ladder to the loft. Dread rose in her like a miasma. "EV! Answer me." She scaled the rungs with Dalton right behind her. In the dim light, there was no sign of EV anywhere. Dalton flicked on the flashlight he had pulled from his pocket and aimed it into the small space. Hay bales, piled to the rafters at the beginning of winter, now only covered part of the floor, which extended several feet past the support poles that ran from floor to roof. Motes of dust and hay particles floated through the beam of light as he played it over the area.

His heart stopped dead then lurched to a pounding crescendo when the light picked out EV's legs sticking out from where her body sprawled behind one of the upright supports. She wasn't moving and he feared the worst.

"No." Chloe shot past him to kneel next to the prone form. Dark blood stained the blue denim covering EV's hip and gleamed wetly from an abrasion the size of a quarter on her forehead. "I think she's been shot." Turning the prisoner over to Horis, Nate vaulted the ladder just in time to see Dalton lay trembling hands against the pulse point on EV's throat. Tears trembled on his lashes when he announced, "She's alive."

Rubbing salty wetness out of her eyes with one hand, Chloe twined the fingers of the others around EV's while Dalton swallowed his own emotions to begin applying first aid.

"Doc Talbot was at The Mudbucket when we left;

someone call and see if we can get him out here. And get everyone with a plow out on the roads. We're going to need an ambulance," Chloe's voice trembled and broke.

"I'm on it." Wesley pulled out his phone to set everything in motion.

"How bad?" Chloe's eyes were dark, fear-filled pools in a face leached of color.

"Looks like the bullet grazed her hip; took a nice chunk of her with it, but I think it looks worse than it is." Whether his words were meant to reassure Chloe or himself, Dalton could not have said. "I think the impact must have spun her around and she bounced her head off that post." He aimed the flashlight to pinpoint a small smear of red while taking a deep breath to let out a little of the abject terror that had swamped him at the sight of EV lying there. "Knocked her out."

Nate knelt to fold an arm around Chloe, and EV started to stir. Her eyes blinked open slowly to focus on the three faces looking down at her and she tried to speak. Barely a whisper came out.

Dalton leaned closer, "Two hundred dollars," EV muttered.

"Shh. Just rest, now." Dalton rubbed her chilled

fingers between his warm palms. To the others he whispered, "She's not lucid."

"I'm fine." EV's voice was a little stronger. "Pay up. Double or nothing, remember? We won the bet." She pulled her hand gently from his to gingerly touch the soreness just above her left eye. "Stupid post got in my way when the gun went off."

Dalton rocked back on his heels and scowled down in response to her weak, but unrepentant grin. The woman was incorrigible. But she was still here, and to him that was all that counted. "You've been shot and all you can think about is that stupid bet."

"The rat bastard shot me?" The struggle to sit up sent EV's head into a pounding mass of pain. "Where? Am I dying?"

Still shaking, Chloe answered, "The bullet grazed your hip, and no, you're not dying. I nearly did when I saw you lying there, but you were lucky."

"It doesn't hurt very much."

"Give it time," Nate's dry tone covered abject relief after several moments of pure panic. "When the adrenaline rush fades, you'll feel it."

"Doc Talbot's on his way," Wesley called up. "He said not to move her until he gets here."

EV wasn't having any of that. "I will not have that

old man climbing up and down a rickety old ladder to look at a bump on the head and a flesh wound. Help me up, Dalton." When he didn't move immediately, she softened her voice, "Please."

Getting down the ladder was more painful than she expected, but walking past Chet Morgan without giving in to the temptation to deliver a swift kick to the side of his head was harder. However, leaning down to catch his eye and deliver the news, "Stacey Hawthorne is awake and talking," was worth every twinge in the hip that was now beginning to burn with pain.

"Is that true?" Wesley demanded.

EV nodded. "Christian called right before we left. She's going to make a full recovery."

"I've felt so guilty for not picking up when she called me the other night. I thought she wanted to talk about getting back together, when all she wanted was my help. Instead, I left her stranded on the side of the road with this maniac." Even if EV didn't get to deliver that kick, Wesley managed one before Nate could pull him back.

Not five minutes after EV was carefully aided down to the barn floor, Doc Talbot walked in with— of all people—Allegra Worth, who carried a bundle that turned out to be some of the afghans Priscilla had slated for donation to a nursing home in Gilmore. While Doc had been getting his things together, she had raided Thread. Without fanfare, Allegra bundled Chloe into one of the colorful blankets and Jessamyn into another. A third she slung over EV's shoulders. The warmth and thoughtfulness went a long way toward easing Chloe's antagonism toward her.

"What kind of trouble have you managed to get into this time, Emmalina Torrence?"

"Nothing a couple painkillers won't cure."

"I'll be the judge of that." With a minimum of fuss, Doc cleaned and dressed the nasty red furrow the bullet had made across her hip, and took a look at the small cut on her forehead, examined her for signs of concussion. "A few stitches and you're going to have one dilly of a headache, but I think you'll do."

The next hour passed in a flurry of activity. More police and an ambulance arrived. Chet Morgan was taken into custody and EV, against her will, went to County. In a choice between getting stitches and having a scar, her insistence on the latter went completely ignored. The only good thing that came out of going to the hospital was the chance it gave her to talk to Stacey Hawthorne. As soon as she was patched up to Doc Talbot's satisfaction, that's exactly where EV, along with Chloe and the others, went.

A very much improved version of Stacey greeted Jessamyn with a happy cry. "You're safe. I've been so worried."

Jessamyn noted the way Christian hovered and the way Stacey let him. They must have played out their own version of While You Were Sleeping; one that might have a happy ending for both of them.

When Nate nudged him, Dalton stepped forward to gently interrogate Stacey. "Can you tell me what you remember about the day you were injured?"

"I got a phone call from one of my former colleagues to tell me Ronald Trafton was dead. Naturally, I called Alicia—Jessamyn—to let her know. It felt fishy to me from the start. When she confirmed that he had a fear of heights, I suspected Ronald might have jumped, and I knew that with him gone, Alicia was in danger. We had kept her name out of everything, so not even Levy was sure she was the one who found the discrepancy. I was on my way to Ponderosa Pines to try and talk her into going into hiding with me for a few days while I put things in motion to get another investigation started. Big Mac has a few key members of D-4 in his pocket, so I had to move carefully."

Nate and Dalton exchanged a look. That much they had figured out on their own.

"You and Alicia were on friendly terms?"

"We got to know each other during the trial, and then after, when bits of information began coming to light that implicated Ronald Trafton as having created the second set of books. I knew he was being set up, and it was only a matter of time before they realized Alicia had been involved, so I advised them both to disappear for a while. Ronald wouldn't go, and they redoubled their efforts toward framing him. Setting him up took the heat off of Levy & Wade, and provided Big Mac a means for getting out of jail."

Putting the pieces together, EV commented, "So, Chet was tracking you in the hopes you would lead him to Alicia."

"Right. When I wouldn't tell him where she was, we fought and I ended up here."

"They sent Chet Morgan to find me, but I was already holed up at Tank's, and since Ronald insisted I stay away from the trial, they didn't have a face or a name." Jessamyn filled in another blank.

"And that's why he kept asking me if I was from

Boston," Chloe said. "He was trying to figure out if I was the woman he was sent to find."

"Then how did he figure out it was me?" Jessamyn frowned.

"You can blame us for that," Nate spoke up. "We gave Tim McReady the name Alicia, and he must be on Big Mac's payroll. I'm betting he followed up at Levy & Wade, got a last name, and ran Alicia Kayden's driver's license. That would give him a photo, which he then sent along to Morgan."

"When he saw me in The Mudbucket, he followed me back to Tank's." Jessamyn picked up the narrative. "The rest, you pretty much already know. I didn't dare even come visit Stacey; it seemed too dangerous. I felt awful."

Stacey smiled reassuringly at her friend. "You did exactly what I would have wanted you to do. Stay safe."

"What's going to happen next?" Christian leaned forward to grasp Stacey's hand, which put a delighted smile on EV's face. "Will they just send more goons, or is everyone safe?"

"Levy was taken into custody about an hour ago amid overwhelming evidence that he was the one who perpetrated the fraud. That should let Alicia off the hook."

Dalton cracked the first smile since he'd seen EV lying motionless in a cloud of hay dust. "That's case closed. Can we all go home, now?"

"Sure. And on the way, we can stop at the ATM so you can settle our bet. Two-hundred dollars." Careful of her injured hip, Dalton slid an arm around EV, leaned down and whispered into her ear, "Double or nothing?"

Chapter 24

When the quiet knock sounded on her door, EV had just settled down with a cup of tea and a good book to take her mind off the incessant itching from her stitches. Soon the wound would heal and she would be back to normal.

Of all the people on the other side of that knock, a sheepish Nate Harper was the last one she expected to see when she pulled open the door.

"Can I run something by you?" Nate asked without preamble.

"Certainly," EV stepped back to let him in. Nate settled at the breakfast bar while EV leaned against the opposite counter—standing hurt less than sitting. "What's on your mind?"

"You think Dalton's doing a good job, right?" Expecting something to do with Chloe, his question threw her off.

"Wouldn't you be the best judge of his ability? My opinion is going to be biased and I can tell the question was rhetorical. Tell me what this is all about."

Nate nodded. "When he applied, I thought he was a little too eager. The eager ones usually wash out at the first crime scene. I thought seeing Luther would send Dalton packing, but he sucked it up and did the job."

Where was this going? EV was beginning to wonder.

"I forced him into taking point on the Stacey Hawthorne case, and he handled it like a seasoned cop—logical, methodical—he stayed with me or ahead of me every step of the way."

Sensing this conversation wasn't shaping up to be the tea and cookies kind, EV offered Nate a beer instead, took one herself, and swigged it right from the bottle. "Is that a problem? Or did you expect to provide him with excellent training and then have him fall on his face?"

"When I came back home, it was supposed to be a temporary assignment."

"If you're going to tell me you want to go back to Portland and break Chloe's heart, I can promise you that shoulder injury will become the least painful thing that's happened to you this year."

Nate's mouth dropped open. "What? No! That's not..." A hand lifted to ruffle through his hair. "You get a lot of exercise jumping to conclusions? I don't want to go back to Portland at all. I went into law enforcement thinking it was my lifelong dream, and realized only recently that I stayed with it mostly to piss off my mother."

The truth didn't surprise EV in the least. Nate's mother had all the tender mercy of a shark in a pool of chum when it came to defending the civil rights of her clients. With her son, though, she hovered and smothered. Nate choosing a career she would hate was not difficult for EV to imagine. Not that you'd ever know it; Barbara Harper expounded her son's virtues any chance she got, leaving the harping for when the two were alone.

"I think I'm getting the picture," she waved a hand to indicate he should continue.

"Ponderosa Pines is too small to need an elevated police presence. The way Dalton has progressed, I'm well on my way to being superfluous." Nate shoved back the stool he had been sitting on to pace the room. "I should be upset by that, but I'm relieved."

She let him talk it out.

"All this, it's giving me a chance to start over—and it's coming at exactly the wrong time." He slumped back down on the stool. "I've just gotten engaged, and now I'm about to go out and try to find myself." A shudder ran through him, "just saying those words makes me want to gouge my own eyes out. It's time for me to settle down, maybe start a family. Not to go off on some existential journey. Chloe says we don't need my income, so I'm free to do whatever I want." The twist of his lips told EV everything she needed to know.

"Chloe's nothing like your mother. She's not trying to gain control over you, she only wants to give you the space to find what makes you happy. You know money isn't her focus. She's good at making it. Not as good as Lila, but she could be if the trading game held any excitement for her. That's not her thing. You are. You dolt." A smile softened the blow.

EV watched the tension drain from Nate's body; his shoulders dropped from their hunched position as the weight he had been carrying fell from them. "I love my mother to the ends of the world and back; I also resent her for trying to control every area of my life. Chloe would never do that, and I didn't make the connection until you pointed it out. You're one hell of a woman, EV Torrence. Dalton's a lucky guy." Nate gained his feet, circled the table to plant a smacking kiss on EV's now-blushing cheek before whistling his way out the door.

Watching him go, EV grinned. If she wasn't mistaken, Nate was about to take a walk on the wild side. Should be fun to see it all play out.

Thanks so much for reading!

We know you're wondering if there's going to be another Ponderosa Pines mystery, and the honest answer is: we hope so. We have a draft in the works, and will try our best to get it to you ASAP! For now, keep reading for previews of our other series.

Quick Author's Note

If you weren't already aware, ReGina and Erin are a mother/daughter writing team, and yes, that means we mix family and work - with all the ups and downs you might expect. It helps that we basically share a single brain most of the time and tend to finish each other's sentences...literally. It also means we sometimes squabble over plot points, but since we're best friends, too, we let that stuff roll right off our backs.

This is the first series we ever wrote together, and it holds a special place in our hearts. Fun fact! In the book, the town's name of Ponderosa Pines came about as a compromise between the couple who founded the town. In reality, it came from the name of the apartment building Erin was living in at the time!

We intended to set the story in a similar apartment complex but as things went along, we ended with something just a bit quirkier. Ponderosa Pines is a place we'd both like to live.

In case you're wondering how we split up the work when we write together, we come up with a plot and scene list and then call dibs on which ones we want to write. In this case, Erin called all of the Chloe scenes while ReGina handled EV. As always, we go over each other's work once the book is done.

Anyway, if you've come this far with us and not decided we're complete and total whackadoodles... and especially if you have, we're offering a chance to sign up for our newsletters— the best place to get new release updates, sales notifications, and other fun content.

You can sign up for ReGina's newsletter here and/or Erin's newsletter here. As a thank-you gift for hanging out with us, you'll also get a FREE novella that isn't available anywhere else. And of course, we promise not to SPAM your inbox!

Love, hugs, and happy reading,
ReGina & Erin

P.S. If you enjoyed this book, it would be great if you could leave a review or recommendation on your favorite store, GoodReads, or BookBub.

Your reviews help indie authors sell more books!

Other Books

If you'd like to meet more people who live rent-free in our heads, here's a list of other series we've written. Our books are all set in fictional towns in Maine, and some characters like to flit back and forth between series. The cast of Psychic Seasons hangs out with Everly and also with Lexi Balefire from the Fate Weaver series. Mag and Clara Balefire are Lexi's grandmother and aunt!

The Psychic Seasons Series
Four women, four love stories, and a whole lot of supernatural surprises. In the quaint town of Oakville, Maine, psychic visions, ghostly whispers, and fate itself conspire to change lives—and hearts—forever

The Haunted Everly After Mysteries

Everly Dupree came home for a fresh start—not a full-time gig solving ghostly murders. But when the dearly departed start demanding justice, what's a reluctant medium to do?

Nell Page: Accidental Investigator
Nell Page owns a bookstore, drinks too much coffee, and has a habit of noticing things she probably shouldn't. With warmth, wit, and an accidental talent for investigating, Nell tackles mysteries that don't always involve murder—but always matter.

Fate Weaver
Lexi Balefire—matchmaker, witch, and accidental fate-weaver—must balance love, magic, and a family legacy of chaos before destiny decides for her!

The Mag and Clara Balefire Mysteries
Sister witches Mag and Clara Balefire move to a sleepy Maine town for a fresh start—only to find themselves conjuring up trouble, solving murders, and keeping their magic under wraps in this charmingly witchy cozy mystery series

Laurel Haven Witches
Four witches, destined by blood and magic, must embrace their power, battle a dark legacy, and surrender to the love that could break the curse—or bind them to it forever.